"Looks like a mighty pretty customer,"

Adam remarked to himself when he first saw Donna Calvert walking toward him in the sunlight. Her red headband was vivid against her dark hair and pale complexion. Her tailored shirt and riding breeches seemed to enhance her femininity. Gold glinted at her ears, and there was a flash of diamonds at her wrist.

"Good morning," he said. "I'm Adam Challow. Can I help you, Ms...."

"Miss Calvert," she said. "I phoned this morning. I was told to come before noon."

"Oh, yes. About the horses? How many horses do you want to board?" Adam asked.

Donna looked at him in surprise. "I don't have any horses."

Adam frowned as her words penetrated. "Then why are you here and dressed for riding?"

"I'm applying for the job you advertised."

"But that was for a farmhand!" he exclaimed. "And frankly," he added, looking her up and down, "I need a *man*."

D0962963

Dear Reader,

At Silhouette Romance we're starting the New Year off right! This month we're proud to present *Donavan,* the ninth wonderful book in Diana Palmer's enormously popular LONG, TALL TEXANS series. *The Taming of the Teen* is a delightful sequel to Marie Ferrarella's *Man Trouble*—and Marie promises that Angelo's story is coming soon. Maggi Charles returns with the tantalizing *Keep It Private* and Jody McCrae makes her debut with the charming *Lake of Dreams.* Pepper Adams's *That Old Black Magic* casts a spell of love in the Louisiana bayou—but watch out for Crevi the crocodile!

Of course, no lineup in 1992 would be complete without our special WRITTEN IN THE STARS selection. This month we're featuring the courtly Capricorn man in Joan Smith's *For Richer, for Poorer.*

Throughout the year we'll be publishing stories of love by all of your favorite Silhouette Romance authors—Diana Palmer, Brittany Young, Annette Broadrick, Suzanne Carey and many, many more. The Silhouette Romance authors and editors love to hear from readers, and we'd love to hear from *you!*

Happy New Year... and happy reading!

Valerie Susan Hayward
Senior Editor

JOAN SMITH

For Richer, for Poorer

Silhouette Romance

Published by Silhouette Books New York

America's Publisher of Contemporary Romance

SILHOUETTE BOOKS
300 E. 42nd St., New York, N.Y. 10017

FOR RICHER, FOR POORER

Copyright © 1992 by Joan Smith

LOVE AND THE CAPRICORN MAN
Copyright © 1992 by Harlequin Enterprises B.V.

ISBN: 0-373-08838-8

First Silhouette Books printing January 1992

Printed in the U.S.A.

Books by Joan Smith

Silhouette Romance

Next Year's Blonde #234
Caprice #255
From Now On #269
Chance of a Lifetime #288
Best of Enemies #302
Trouble in Paradise #315
Future Perfect #325
Tender Takeover #343
The Yielding Art #354
The Infamous Madam X #430
Where There's a Will #452

Dear Corrie #546
If You Love Me #562
By Hook or By Crook #591
After the Storm #617
Maybe Next Time #635
It Takes Two #656
Thrill of the Chase #669
Sealed with a Kiss #711
Her Nest Egg #755
Her Lucky Break #795
For Richer, for Poorer #838

JOAN SMITH

"I inherited Leo's energy in full measure. I am used to doing two jobs at once, i.e., raising a family of three children and teaching French and English, or writing. Since I have written aproximately one hundred books, I guess I can lay claim to Leo's inventiveness as well. I love the arts and dabble in both painting and sculpting. Some Leos have clairvoyant abilities. I do seem to have a 'seventh' sense where my children are concerned, especially if they are in trouble. But that may be due to the fact that I am a seventh daughter.

"My marriage to a Cancer should not be as harmonious as it is, but the stars only incline, they do not compel. My husband and I share many common interests, especially family and home-related ones such as cooking and gardening."

CAPRICORN

Tenth sign of the Zodiac
December 23 to January 20
Symbol: Goat
Planet: Saturn
Element: Earth
Stone: Garnet, Onyx
Color: Black
Metal: Lead
Flower: Carnation
Lucky Day: Saturday
Countries: India, Mexico, Afghanistan
Cities: Oxford, Delhi, Brussels

Famous Capricorns

Martin Luther King, Jr.　　Marlene Dietrich
Benjamin Franklin　　Joan of Arc
Elvis Presley　　Mary Tyler Moore
Cary Grant　　Ava Gardner

★

Chapter One

Donna Calvert unlocked her mailbox and drew out one lonesome letter. Her heart skipped a beat when she saw the long envelope with the words Unicorn Publishing Company in the upper left-hand corner. As soon as she felt the weight of paper within, she knew her story was being returned—again—and her eagerness subsided. An acceptance letter wouldn't be so heavy. She took the mail to the table, opened the long envelope and read,

Dear Ms. Calvert:
We are sorry, but because of the number of articles submitted to us, we are unable to send a personal reply.

Not even a personal rejection, but a form letter.

At times like this she felt her dream of becoming a writer was doomed. The story she'd submitted was a good one.

What did they expect in two thousand words, *Gone With the Wind?*

The kitchen door opened, and her cousin, Jeanie Calvert, came into the room, her high heels tapping. Jeanie's fashionable dress and blond hair were in sharp contrast to Donna's casual appearance. Jeanie's face was made up for work. Donna felt like a frump beside her, but a writer had to be comfortable, and no one would see her crouched over her typewriter from eight until noon.

"Is that the mail?" Jeanie asked, pouring a cup of coffee and sitting at one end of the kitchen table that served double duty as Donna's desk.

"Yeah, another rejection," Donna said, and sighed. "That darned story has been to New York and back more often than I have."

Jeanie gave a rueful smile. "Don't give up, girl. Some of the most successful books were turned down *dozens* of times before they were accepted." She pulled the newspaper forward and opened it. "It figures," she snorted. "Your horoscope today warns that a favorite project might fail. Your planets must be in adverse aspect."

"Doesn't it say anything good?" Donna asked glumly.

"A good day for romance," Jeanie said, looking up with a grin.

"I'm not interested in romance at the moment. What I need is money. Half days at the supermarket hardly pay room and board. It wouldn't do that if Uncle Mike hadn't given us this apartment at a bargain-basement price. Of course, it *is* a basement apartment," she added, glancing up at the dusty half window near the ceiling, where sunlight streaked down on the sink.

"I don't know why you don't ask Mike to find you something at the paper," Jeanie said. "I'm sure he could find a spot for you, like he did for me."

"He didn't have an opening for a journalist, Jeanie. You're great at selling advertising. I'd be lousy at it."

"You mean you didn't want to ask him," Jeanie translated. "I keep telling you, you don't put yourself forward enough. You're the same with guys. You never take the initiative. You just curl up with that typewriter and live life vicariously."

"Most writers are introverts," Donna said. "It goes with the territory."

"Anybody who didn't know you're shy would think you were a snob," Jeanie continued. "Shy is bad enough, but you cover it up by acting so cool."

"So sue me," Donna snorted. "I never had your knack for putting myself forward. It makes me feel uncomfortable. I want to write, not sell advertising."

"You're a Gemini. You should be versatile," Jeanie pointed out. She buttered a bran muffin and bit into it.

"You know us Geminis—versatile and ambitious, but sometimes visionary. My vision is to be a writer."

"I'm sure Mike would find you something in the writing department if you'd ask."

"Beg, you mean. I know how thinly Uncle Mike spreads his reporters. They have to go report on council meetings and baseball games at night, as well as work all day. It wouldn't leave me any time for my own writing. I *do* need more money though. Pass the want ads, will you?"

Jeanie slid the newspaper ads across the table, and Donna hastily ran her eye down the columns. "Hey, look at this!" she exclaimed. "Samara is advertising for summer help. Isn't Samara that big horse farm on Highway 37? I love riding! We took lessons back home and rode at college. I even have my outfit here."

"Samara isn't a horse farm. It's a regular farm that just boards horses on the side. They probably want somebody to drive a tractor or something," Jeanie said vaguely.

"If Samara boards horses, then they have to have somebody look after them. I'm going to give it a shot."

"Why not? It's worth a try. And as you often say, a writer needs all kinds of different experiences."

The girls exchanged hopeful smiles. Despite the differences in their personalities, Jeanie and Donna were as close as sisters. They had both been raised in Buffalo, attended the same schools and later the same college. When they had graduated and gone looking for work, it was Jeanie who'd had the idea of applying to the patriarch of their family, Mike Calvert, who ran a newspaper in Bayville, a town in upstate New York. Bayville was close to home, but living there gave them the freedom of being on their own.

Mike Calvert was the brother of both their fathers. He probably could have found a corner for Donna at his newspaper, or in his large real estate development company. But Donna was sensitive; she wouldn't feel right being shoehorned in where she wasn't needed, possibly causing hard feelings among his other employees.

The basement apartment they rented from him had formerly been occupied by the janitor, but when Mike Calvert put up another building next door, he hired its janitor to handle both buildings. With more ingenuity and work than money, the girls had transformed the dark space into livable quarters. Their uncle had provided paint for the walls, and they had done the work. Posters, prints and plants were their main decoration. Jeanie supplied the modern art posters, Donna the prints, and they both binged on plants to fill the empty spaces.

Jeanie finished her muffin and stood up, glancing at her watch. "I gotta go. Take the van. It has half a tank of gas. Good luck at Samara."

One of the perks Jeanie enjoyed at the *Bayville Beacon* was the use of a company car that consistently ran. The battered little van that the cousins had bought with the money from their combined graduation presents only worked when it felt like it. It disliked rainy days, but today the sun was shining, so Donna felt it would get her to Samara.

She glanced at her watch. Eight-fifteen was too early to call. She would phone at nine and make an appointment. That left her forty-five minutes to devote to her writing. If she got hired at Samara, she would quit the afternoon supermarket job, work on the farm all day and do her writing at night.

Deeply involved in her work, she could hardly believe that three-quarters of an hour had passed when she glanced at the clock. She called Samara. A woman answered and told her to come out before noon. A Mr. Challow would see her.

The next problem was what to wear. Presumably a farm worker would wear jeans and sneakers, but to apply for a job, she felt she should wear something dressier. She flipped through her wardrobe, rejecting dresses as too dressy and jeans as too casual. Her eye fell on her tan riding breeches. Samara had dozens of horses, even if it didn't breed them. Jodhpurs were neat and stylish, without being formal.

She undressed and slid into them. Riding breeches naturally suggested riding boots. Anything else looked funny, so she struggled into her riding boots. Now for a top. Since she was going for an interview, she wanted to wear something better than a T-shirt and chose a white tailored shirt.

Before leaving, she went to the bathroom mirror to brush her hair. In the poor light from one lamp, her chestnut hair looked almost black against her fair skin. She wore it short in summer, brushed back casually. The humidity increased its natural tendency to curl and lent her a tousled look. She twisted a scarlet bandanna into a ribbon and used it as a hair band. That was better. Her face stood out, its high cheekbones emphasized. The small gold hoop earrings lent a gypsy touch, without being gaudy. She was a woman, after all. She also left on the bracelet Jeanie had given her for her birthday. Jeanie, who was deeply involved in fashion, said it was a tennis bracelet. It was a slender circlet of imitation diamonds, which seemed like a strange thing to wear while playing tennis, but Jeanie would know.

The only makeup Donna wore in the daytime was lipstick and a touch of eyeliner, to emphasize her wide-set, dark blue eyes. When she had applied her makeup, she stepped away from the mirror. As an afterthought, she decided to take her riding helmet, in case Mr. Challow asked to see a sample of her riding.

Walking out into the brilliant sunlight from the basement apartment was like going from night to day. Donna's spirits lifted as a breeze riffled her hair. The pinging and rattling of the van sounded like a one-man band when the motor engaged, but at least it started on the first try.

Soon she had left town and was on Highway 37, headed into the countryside. A feeling of serenity descended on her as she drove past green pastures, where holsteins grazed lazily in the sun. Farming was such a peaceful sort of life. When she was a kid, she had spent a part of several summers on her grandmother's farm. By the time she was in high school, she no longer wanted to be parted from her friends for long, but her farm memories were happy ones.

Wrapped up in memories, Donna nearly missed her turnoff. A wrought-iron gate between stone pillars stood open. The word Samara was written in scrolled iron on an arch above the doors. Beneath the letters, a set of giant maple keys seemed suspended in air, but were attached by a narrow band to the gate frame. Tall maples grew along the front of the property, providing shade and privacy. Stately poplars formed a fence along the driveway leading to the farm. She turned the van into the graveled lane.

Funny she didn't see any horses... Samara's property must lie on the other side of the house. She peered to the right as she drove up the poplar-shaded road, and did see a few kids riding horses in a field. At the end of the drive a large brick house loomed. As she drew nearer, she saw an elegant Georgian doorway with a fanlight and flanked by pillars. Black shutters spread at either side of the gleaming windows. It looked like a very profitable farm.

She parked her car under a spreading maple tree and sat regarding the front door. Should she go there or around to the back? Presumably the owner would be at work in the middle of the morning. She always dreaded the moment of meeting new people. She must remember what Jeanie had said, and not act standoffish. She didn't feel she'd have much trouble that way with a farmer. In fact, it was mostly when meeting eligible men that she felt uncomfortable.

She picked up her riding helmet, and with it dangling from her fingers, she walked around to the rear. The largest barn she had ever seen rose up like a mountain before her. Her grandmother's barn had been one of gray weathered wood. This one was painted a deep red. Large double doors stood open and revealed the shadow of two men moving within.

She strode forward at a faster pace, her long legs moving easily in her low heels. "Hi, I'm looking for Mr. Challow," she called, waving to attract attention.

The shorter of the two men said, "Looks like another customer, Adam."

"And a mighty pretty one," Adam Challow replied. The deep baritone of his voice held an edge of interest.

What he first saw was how the sunlight glinted on the woman's dark hair, pale face and white shirt. Gold glinted at her ears. Her severe shirt and riding breeches seemed to enhance her femininity. Adam watched with interest as she advanced, noticing the sway of her hips, her tiny waist and the slight jiggle inside her shirt.

Her outfit and the helmet dangling from her fingers suggested she was a horsewoman, come to board her horse at his stable. Adam only did this as a sideline, to maximize the use of his land and barns until he had them totally filled with holsteins. In fact, the running of the horse farm was done by a neighbor, Mrs. McAllister. He actually considered the horsey set a nuisance, but there were some very pretty women among them.

"Good morning," he said, advancing to shake her hand. "I'm Adam Challow. Can I help you, Miss—" He cast a surreptitious glance at her left hand. No wedding band. He noticed the flash of "diamonds" at her wrist. He had seen those bracelets before on the wealthy riders. He wondered how many horses she wanted to board.

"Miss Calvert," she said, smiling as she offered her hand.

"Calvert!" The name was like a red flag to Adam Challow. She was one of *them!* Mike Calvert was one gigantic pain in the neck to the farmers. Not satisfied with littering his ugly apartment buildings all over Bayville, he was now encroaching into the countryside, driving up the cost of farmland and making it impossible for farmers to expand. He had outbid a friend of Adam's on a nearby farm, which suggested that Calvert was planning to build one of his monstrosities out this way, despite the zoning laws.

On the other hand, this young woman certainly didn't bear any physical resemblance to that blimp of a Mike. "Any kin to Mike Calvert?" he asked.

Wearing the name Calvert seemed to open a few doors in Bayville, but somehow Donna didn't think it impressed this man much. She had to wonder at the sudden freezing of his smile. "A poor relation," she replied.

"I didn't realize any of the Calverts were poor," he said in a tight voice.

"We learn something new every day," she replied, and forced a smile, since she wanted the job.

"I figure I already know quite a bit about the Calverts," Adam said, narrowing his eyes.

Donna felt a tingle of annoyance at both his tone and his blatant assessment of her body. Adam Challow looked as if he had just swaggered out of a western movie. Maybe it was the wide-brimmed hat tipped over his eye that first gave that impression, because he wasn't wearing chaps or cowboy boots. The blue-and-white checked shirt hugging his broad shoulders managed to look both macho and elegant at the same time. His long legs were encased in faded blue jeans, and on his feet—a size twelve at least—he wore work boots.

Donna decided it was his face that made her think of old cowboy heroes. It was the weathered brown of oak wood, a chiseled face, with a strong nose and jaw. The jet-black sideburns below his hat suggested his hair color, and a black slash of eyebrows confirmed it. His eyes were smoky gray, with long lashes that softened the severe look Donna saw in them.

"I guess most people around here know Mike," she said.

Adam figured that if this woman was a Calvert, then she was probably loaded. It amused him to think of making money from a Calvert, and he smiled. When he spoke, his voice had softened, but it wasn't a silky voice. It was like wool, soft and warm, but with a rough edge. "What can I do for you, Miss Calvert?"

"I phoned you this morning. I was told to come any time before noon."

"Oh, yes, about the horses?" he said. Mrs. McAllister handled the phone calls.

"That's right. Where do you keep them? I didn't see any as I drove out."

"I'll show you the facilities," he said, motioning toward a barn. Not the huge red one, but a smaller one off to the right.

"I've been riding for quite a few years," Donna said, to win his approval.

"How many horses do you have, Miss Calvert? Is it just the one, or—"

She stopped and looked at him in surprise. "I don't *have* any horses," she said, and laughed nervously.

Adam was noticing how big and lustrous her eyes were, and how her laughter tinkled like a silver bell. He *didn't* notice, for a moment, what she said. When her words penetrated, he frowned in confusion. "Then why are you here, and dressed for riding?" he asked.

"I'm applying for the job you advertised in the *Beacon*. I phoned earlier."

Adam stood still, blinking his eyes. "But that was for a farmhand," he exclaimed. Farm workers were hard to come by. Usually he was lucky to get two or three applicants, always men, never dressed to the nines as this woman was.

"Oh. I thought it might be for the riding stable. I guess you do regular farming, too."

"You could say that," Adam said rather grimly. Typical of these town folks not to have heard of his award-winning herd!

"I'm willing to give it a try. I'm versatile. I spent several summers on a farm when I was a kid," she added.

His eyes flickered over her spotless white shirt and polished boots. "I don't think you're exactly the worker I had in mind. I'm looking for a man. Sorry, Miss Calvert." He turned and began retracing his steps to the cow barn. Bloody waste of time! His top hand came out of the barn and stood, waiting to speak to Adam.

Donna had to run to keep up with Adam's long strides. "Is it just because I'm a woman?" she demanded angrily, surprised at her own daring. But something about this man made her forget all about being shy.

Next she'd be reporting him to some equal rights board. He stopped and stood, arms akimbo. "No, ma'am. I wasn't advertising for somebody to exercise the horses. Mrs. McAllister handles that business. I run a dairy farm. I need somebody to help set up the milking machines and clean them when the milking's done. Someone who can handle the feed and water. Somebody who knows cows and can spot when one is not well. Somebody who can run a tractor and fill the hayloft, get the cows out in the morning and in at night. Can you do that?"

"No," she admitted, "but I could learn. Some of it, anyway. Looking after a herd of cows can't be that complicated."

Adam stared at her as he heard his complex and highly scientific life's work diminished. An amateur could learn it in no time, while *he* had studied for years at an agricultural college and spent the whole of his life on the job. He stomped quickly on to the barn, with Donna trailing behind.

The man who was waiting came forward and nudged Adam's elbow. "What is it, Joe?" Adam asked irritably. Joe smiled at Donna and offered his hand. "This is Joe Fraser. Miss Calvert."

"How do you do?" She glanced at the rangy young man. He was tall, thin, with sandy hair and a loose smile. He looked to be about twenty-seven.

"Miss Calvert rides, and spent a vacation on a farm when she was a child. She wants a job," Adam said, his voice heavy with sarcasm.

Joe listened, then said, "With all the new calves to be bottle-fed—twenty-five of them—even an untrained hand would be better than nothing, Adam."

"I can do that!" Donna said eagerly. She had done this at her grandmother's farm and enjoyed it.

"That's hardly a full-time job," Adam objected.

"I'm not necessarily looking for a full-time job," she said. "Just mornings, preferably," she added, figuring that she could keep the afternoon job at the supermarket. "I do know something about cows."

Joe and Adam exchanged a questioning look. They both knew Joe was wasting his valuable time bottle-feeding the twenty-five new calves. No one else had applied. Right now even an interested greenhorn would be better than nothing. Adam thought it might be amusing to give Miss Calvert a lesson in how the other half lived. Her cavalier remark that his work couldn't be that complicated still stung. She obviously didn't need the money, since she was willing to settle for half days. Just why was she here?

While he stood undecided, Joe said, "There are a few odd jobs that a woman could do. The fences need painting, for instance. I don't see any reason Miss Calvert couldn't drive the lawn tractor. There's a full acre of lawn to cut every week."

Adam looked uncertainly at the applicant. She certainly seemed eager, which was odd. Was old Mike up to something? Sending a spy in to gauge his financial vulnerability? "How did you come to apply here?" he asked suspiciously. "If you want work, why not work for Mike Calvert?"

"He didn't need help, and I didn't want to impose."

"There must be more suitable work in town. A fashion shop," he suggested, examining her outfit.

"I'd rather be outdoors," she said. One store job was more than enough.

She was awfully pretty, and seemed enthusiastic. "I really don't think this will work out, Miss Calvert, but if you want to give it a try for a few days, be my guest. I pay beginners minimum wages."

Her eyes sparkled with pleasure. "Great! Can I start tomorrow?"

"Yes, at six-thirty," he replied, and watched as her jaw fell. "You realize, of course, from your past experience, that farmers rise with the sun."

"Of course," she said, in a weak voice. Six-thirty! She'd never make it.

"I suggest you wear old clothes, if you have any," he said, using it as an excuse to again scrutinize her. "Jeans and a rough shirt will do, and, of course, steel-toed boots," he added.

"Steel-toed boots?" Those were for construction workers. She decided Adam was making fun of her. "Why?"

Joe answered. "Cows are heavy. They don't always watch where they're going."

"You might want to leave your diamonds at home as well," Adam suggested, his lips twitching in amusement.

Donna frowned in confusion, then happened to glance at her bracelet. "Oh, this," she laughed. "It's not valuable. Is there anything else I should know?"

"Be on time," Adam said. "And if you change your mind after considering it, I would appreciate it if you'd let me know. This is just a trial run, you understand. We'll give it till the end of the week. If either of us is not satisfied, that's it."

Donna listened, and when he stopped, she said with more confidence than she felt, "You'll be satisfied. I'm a hard worker." She'd decided she would master the job if it killed her, and show this overbearing jock a lesson.

Adam doubted their ideas of what constituted hard work were the same, but he had said his piece. He'd try her for a week.

"See you tomorrow at six-thirty, then," he said. He tipped his hat and swaggered away. Joe smiled his farewell and went with Adam.

Donna left, satisfied that she had been given a chance, even if Adam Challow did expect her to fail.

"Weren't you kind of hard on the young lady, Adam?" Joe asked.

Adam tossed up his hands. "I must be crazy! Why did I let you talk me into this? She's a Calvert."

"She can't help that. If you don't want to have the bother of looking after her, I'll show her around."

One black eyebrow rose in amusement. "Big of you!" Adam said, and laughed.

Donna reached Bayville in plenty of time to have lunch and still make it to her afternoon job. She even had time to look for a pair of steel-toed boots. She couldn't find any small enough to fit, however, and decided she'd have to make do with her winter boots, since she wasn't going to sacrifice her expensive riding boots. She half suspected that Adam was just giving her a hard time suggesting the steel-toed boots, anyway. If he thought she would be such a poor worker, why had he hired her?

After work Donna brought a pizza home from the supermarket for dinner. It had to be baked, and while the tantalizing aroma of pepperoni and doughy bread filled the kitchen, she made a salad and Jeanie set the table.

"How'd the interview go?" Jeanie asked.

"Funny—different. I think Adam Challow thinks I'm a wimp or something, but he's giving me a week's probation."

"Lucky you! You'll be riding and working with horses all day, and getting paid for it."

"Actually, it's cows I'll be working with. You were right. He's a dairy farmer." Jeanie couldn't quite stifle a giggle. "I think I'll go to the library tonight and see if I can find anything on the subject. I don't want to look like a complete ignoramus. He's just waiting for me to do something stupid."

"I'll go with you. I'm fresh out of reading material."

The pizza was ready, and while they ate, Jeanie said, "By the way, Cousin Matt's coming to visit Mike next week."

"You're kidding! Matt Hibbert, the practically famous writer?" Matt was more famous among his family than the world at large. He had had two scripts taken for television. One of them was being done as a pilot for a possible series, and the network had hired him to do some writing and consultation. Jeanie and Donna had only met Matt at occasional family parties when they were growing up. They'd followed his career with interest.

"Who else? You'll have to get together with him, Donna. He might be able to help you out."

"Wow! Wouldn't it be great to sell a script to television? That story that keeps thumping back in the mail—it'd make a great TV movie."

"Uncle Mike's having a party to show Matt off. We're invited," Jeanie said, smiling to see her cousin so excited.

"What kind of a party?"

"A big one, at the country club. It's Mike and Dora's twenty-fifth anniversary, too, but he wasn't planning to hire the country club for only that. You know Mike—he likes to brag about the family's successes."

"Matt isn't even really a Calvert. I mean he's Aunt Dora's cousin or something, isn't he?"

"Her sister's son. Mike says he knows all the movie stars. Well, some of them, anyway. He's a Sagittarius. Sexy," she said, wiggling her eyebrows. "Speaking of horoscopes, did you fall into any interesting romances today?"

"Nope."

"What about Adam Challow? Is he cute?"

"No, he's gorgeously handsome, and about as romantic as one of his cows. Or bulls. I guess he must be a Taurus," she said.

"Kind and gentle, unless you provoke them."

"I didn't provoke him. On the contrary, he provoked me."

"Headstrong, the Tauruses. Furious when aroused."

"I didn't arouse him, either," she said.

Jeanie laughed at this ambiguous word. "It's early days yet. Maybe you should wear something sexy to work."

"Yeah, like steel-toed boots."

By the time they got to the library, Donna had changed her mind about reading up on cows. She got a book on writing screenplays instead. Geminis, as she well knew, were versatile.

Chapter Two

The sun was barely peeping over the horizon when Donna was awakened by the shrill pealing of her alarm clock the next morning. She had assembled her clothes the night before, and scrambled into her jeans, a pink T-shirt, white athletic socks and her winter boots. They were tan leather, tied in front, and came up to her ankles. She feared their heavy clumping noise would wake Jeanie. She'd leave them at the front door tonight, and put them on as she left tomorrow morning. Six o'clock was much too early to think of eating anything. She just made coffee to wake her up and went out to the van.

It was strangely peaceful having the road to herself, watching the purple horizon of the sky lighten to peach and crimson. Almost like another world. She opened the windows to listen to the sound of birdsong coming from the trees and air around her. The smell of sweet clover took her back to her grandmother's farm. She only met two cars, and she passed a farm tractor that was moving slowly on the road ahead of her. It pulled over, she tooted her thanks, and the driver waved a friendly hand.

Already the wrought-iron gates of Samara had meaning for her when she turned in at the poplar-lined drive. The lane was shady, but sunlight dappled the emerald lawn that stretched on either side. She drove around to the rear, where she had noticed a yellow station wagon parked the day before, because she didn't want to leave the shabby van in front of this gorgeous house. Its ancient brick facade glowed a welcome.

The backyard was empty, but she could see signs of life in the barn beyond, and went inside. Joe Fraser came out wearing a big smile. "You're sure punctual, Miss Calvert," he said.

"Call me Donna." Joe didn't hide his approval, which put Donna at ease.

"I will if you call me Joe."

"You've got a deal. Where do I start, Joe?"

"First we've got to feed the calves. You can fill the milk bottles and begin right away. Follow me."

She followed him through an opening into the milking area, where a row of holsteins were lined up, in the process of being milked by machine. At close range, she was always surprised at their girth, their sleekly swelling sides. Soft music filled the air.

"You like Chopin?" she asked, surprised.

"I prefer rock myself, but the girls like Chopin," he said, smiling, so that she thought he must be joking.

"I had a dog at home that was crazy about Elvis," she said.

"He must have been a hound dog, huh? But I'm serious about the music. It soothes the girls. A contented cow gives more milk."

"Gee, my grandmother never played music to her cows."

"I reckon you'll find a few things have changed from the old days."

Two large tin cans with spouts had been filled with milk and set aside. Donna began using the milk to fill the bottles while Joe told her how much milk to give each calf. "They're up to a quart per feeding now. One bottle each. We'll have to increase it as time goes on. These ladies'll be drinking from the bucket before a cat can twitch its whiskers."

When she had filled the first two bottles and put on the nipples, Joe led her to the area where the calves were penned, ready for breakfast.

"Oh, aren't they adorable!" she squealed, and ran forward, ducking under the barrier to touch the silky head of the closest one. "Just look at those eyelashes. They sure don't need mascara."

A long, rough tongue came out and licked her hand. It felt like sandpaper on her skin, and she snatched her hand away, yelping in surprise, although it didn't hurt.

"They won't bite. They only have teeth on the bottom," a deep voice behind her said. Turning, she saw Adam Challow watching her. He wore a sardonic smile. He had his hat in his hand. His crisp black hair was ruler-straight.

The calves, alerted to the presence of food, began pushing and shoving against her, reaching for the bottles. "One at a time, you guys!" she exclaimed, trying to free herself. The eager animals soon had her surrounded. She looked in rising panic to Adam, barely quelling down the word "Help!"

"Those 'guys' are girls, except for Rambo," Adam said, grinning at her predicament.

They all looked alike to Donna. "Which one's Rambo?" she asked.

"Cattle are like people. The males have different plumbing." His smoky eyes taunted her. "That one's Rambo," he said, pointing to one of the calves near the rear.

Then he took pity on her and pushed the calves aside to free her. "I suggest you lead two at a time over there," he said, pointing to a bench in a corner, "or you'll be stampeded. The girls don't have very good manners."

She ducked under the barrier, unfastened it, and two calves quickly darted out, their hungry mouths reaching for the bottles in her hand. The calves followed her to the spot Adam had indicated. She set one bottle aside. The two calves began pushing and shoving at the bottle she kept in her hand.

"You have two hands," Adam said.

"I'm not ambidextrous."

"I thought you'd done this before?"

She gave a silent glare, picked up the other bottle and pointed it at the calf. Really, that was all there was to it. The calves did the rest, each seizing a nipple and demolishing the quart of milk so quickly she could hardly believe it.

Adam stood watching her. She realized he was looking for flaws and set her mind to her job. "It'll save time if I carry the milk cans here, instead of going there to fill the bottles each time," she said.

"Sounds like a good idea. And keep the cans out of sight or you'll distract the girls from the bottles. They're greedy."

She turned to leave, and the two calves trotted after her. "Stay here," she said. They mooed and began licking at the empty bottles.

She walked back to the barrier and said, "In you go," in a hearty voice. The calves just looked at her with their big brown eyes. She was acutely aware of Adam's gaze, measuring her awful lack of expertise. She was not stupid, however, and realized that they would follow her lead, so she lifted the barrier and joined the other calves. The two who had been fed followed. She slipped out, closed the barrier and gave Adam a pert smile.

"You're learning," he admitted, and went with her to carry one milk can. She hadn't realized milk was so heavy. Her arm felt as if it was being torn from its socket, but she wouldn't satisfy him by complaining. She filled two more bottles, then headed back to retrieve two more calves.

"I'll be all right now, Mr. Challow. I imagine you have more important things to do than watch me," she said, hoping to be rid of him.

"Nothing is more important to me than the welfare of my herd. That depends on my employees, so you're important, too." His eyes flickered down to her feet. "I see you're not wearing proper boots. Watch out for your toes. Even a calf can do damage. When you run into trouble, you can call Joe."

She gave a mutinous stare. "Thanks. *If* I have any trouble, I'll call Joe."

"He'll be in the milking area for a while. You can give him a hand cleaning the cows' udders and purging the milk line when you're done here."

The calves became impatient waiting for their milk. One of them jostled close to her and placed a heavy foot on her toes. It hurt, but not enough to make her fear for her bones. She managed not to yell, but she shoved at the animal's hindquarters. It didn't bulge an inch. She hoped Adam didn't notice what was happening. She let the calves drink from the bottles as though nothing was wrong.

"This is Flossie," Adam said, rubbing the flank of the calf on his right.

Donna tried to extract her foot. "How do you tell them apart? They all look so much alike."

"Each one has different markings. Flossie has that black patch over her eye, like a pirate."

"She should be called Long John Silver—except that's a man's name, of course."

"I only keep the girls—the heifers," he said, looking at them with satisfaction.

She tried once more to move the calf without alerting Adam that she was in pain. "What do you do with the male calves? Surely all the calves aren't obliging enough to be females?"

"I get rid of them," he said.

She came to attention. "You mean you kill them?"

"A male calf is no good to a dairy farmer. I sell them, usually for slaughter, but occasionally I keep one for breeding. I'm keeping Rambo awhile to see how he shapes up. He comes from good stock. The others had to go."

"But that's—" His face assumed a cynical expression. She knew he was just waiting for her to protest, and he would point out that she probably enjoyed veal. "That's interesting," she said, trying to sound unconcerned.

Adam reached out and took one of the bottles she was holding. He held it a few feet away from the calf that was standing on her foot, and the calf immediately came forward to grab the nipple again.

Adam's grin told her he had known all along that she was pinned to the earth by that darned heifer's weight. "You'll find the best way to get them to do what you want is by bribery. Feed them, and they'll follow you anywhere. You *will* see about getting those steel-toed boots, Miss Calvert?"

"I couldn't find any that fit," she said sulkily.

"Is your foot all right? Not in pain?"

She wiggled her toes around. "It seems okay."

"Good. I'll leave you to it now. Just one word of advice, don't turn your back on Rambo. He has the idea he's a battering ram. You're doing fine."

She was pleasantly surprised at this word of commendation, coming after her series of blunders. "Thanks, Mr. Challow."

"We're not formal here. All my employees call me Adam."

"You can call me Donna."

"See you later, Donna." He lifted his hat an inch and left.

She admired his broad shoulders as he strode away, with a gait that would have done justice to John Wayne. She finished feeding the twenty-five calves and went back to help Joe. He showed her how to clean the cows' udders. "We use this mild antiseptic," he said, pouring a liquid into a cup. "You just dip the udders in here."

Feeding the calves was more fun, but she was obliged to help him. "Adam said maybe you'd show me how to clean up the milking machine," she mentioned.

"First we'll get the ladies out to pasture. It's such a fine day we want to take advantage of it. Best get yourself a prod, Donna. They can be stubborn."

A few long sticks were leaning against the wall. Joe took one, she took the other, and they began herding the cattle out of the barn.

"Leave Fifi and Denise behind," he said, when she went to open their barriers. "They're being dried out for insemination. We don't want them stuffing themselves with grass." The two cows set up a loud complaint.

"How do you go about drying the milk up, Joe?"

"You cut back on the feed and milking. Nature takes it from there. They get a bit surly, so you don't want to have too much to do with them."

They led the cattle along to the west pasture. Joe didn't hesitate to give them a sharp rap with his prod if they disobeyed, but Donna just used hers to press against them if they went the wrong way. When the cows were locked in the meadow, they returned to the barn, where Joe showed her how to purge the milk lines.

"You realize this is just a summer job?" Joe asked. "There's more work in summer. Adam always hires a few extras."

"I didn't plan to make a career of it. What I really want to do is write. As soon as I start selling, I'll do that full-time. Meanwhile, I have to eat. Are you a career farmer?"

"My dad owns a dairy farm that's smaller than this. I'll inherit it one day. Right now, I'm working for Adam to learn the latest technology. He's getting a fantastic yield from his herd. He started the local breeding syndicate. It's making a pretty good profit. You'd be surprised what it costs for a first-rate insemination. And of course when he sells one of his prize-winning herd, he makes a million or so."

Donna took that figure for a playful exaggeration. "That much! Holy cow!"

"Yup."

They filled the water troughs and did a few chores in the barn before going back outside. Joe took her on a walking tour of the farm, showing her where the hay and alfalfa were grown, and other produce for the home garden. She was especially interested in the horses, but he didn't venture into the barn. It seemed Mrs. McAllister was very strict in that respect. They just watched the students who were being instructed.

"Funny the way the students hop up and down in the saddle as if they were jumping beans," Joe said.

"That's called English style," Donna replied.

As the morning wore on, Donna began to feel hunger pangs. She hadn't eaten breakfast, and she wasn't used to so much physical labor. Her winter boots made her feet hot. You couldn't work in a barn with cows without picking up a certain amount of dirt, and what she really wanted was a shower, a change of clothes and a huge meal. But as they stood at the fence, watching the cows and their calves grazing, she felt a certain peace and satisfaction.

Joe told her some of their names. Brigitte, Cecile, Yvonne.

"Why does he use so many French names?' she asked.

"Mrs. Challow usually gives them their names. She's from France."

She looked at him in surprise. Mrs. Challow! "I didn't know he was married!" Then she blushed. That outburst sounded as if she were disappointed. Maybe she was, a little. Adam wasn't particularly friendly, but he was certainly handsome.

Joe gave her a knowing smile. "That's Adam's mother I'm talking about. She was a French war bride. She and Adam's dad started this farm. Sometimes she joins us for coffee breaks. Which is just about now," he said, looking at his watch.

"I didn't bring anything, and I'm starving," she said in dismay. "I didn't eat any breakfast. I never thought of bringing a snack. I never had a job like this before, cut off from restaurants and everything. I'll bring a thermos tomorrow."

"Coffee's provided gratis. There's a picnic table on the patio. We'll go along there now."

Behind the house there was a large stone patio, concealed by a privacy hedge. When they went through the archway, Donna saw a kidney-shaped pool glimmering like a jewel in the sunlight. This farm really had all the luxuries! The patio was surrounded with pretty red geraniums. On the shady side next to the house, ferns moved lazily in the breeze. Next to the picnic table was a white iron table and half a dozen chairs. The shade provided by a tall maple was welcome as the sun was rising high overhead.

"Eddie and Luke are repairing the fences today," Joe said. "Looks like it'll just be you and me."

As he spoke, the back door opened and a young woman with a ponytail came out bearing a tray with a coffeepot, cups and a plate with a serviette over it. Joe introduced her as Debbie Jackson.

"I'd like to wash up," Donna said.

Joe answered, "There's a tap by the side of the house. We can't cart all this dirt into the kitchen. Debbie'd kill us."

"You better believe it," Debbie agreed. "I got enough to do without washing the floor twice a day."

"Debbie helps Mrs. Challow around the house," Joe explained.

He showed Donna where the tap was, and they both washed their faces and hands. When they returned to the patio, Debbie was just pouring three cups of coffee. Donna thought, from that third cup, that Debbie was joining them.

"Adam's back, is he?" Joe said to her.

"He's on the phone. He'll be right out, Joe." As Debbie chatted to them for a few minutes, Donna noticed she was older than she looked at first glance. She wore a wedding ring, and when Joe asked her about "the kids," she assumed she was also a mother.

"I made your favorite today, Joe," Debbie said. "Carrot muffins. No icing, though. You don't want to lose your girlish figure."

When she was passed the plate, Donna had trouble restricting herself to one muffin. They were nice fat muffins, stuffed with raisins and walnuts and hot from the oven. The smell was tantalizing, and the taste lived up to the smell. "These are delicious, Debbie!" she said. "And I am *starved!* I could eat the whole plate."

The kitchen door opened and Adam stepped out. "Save one for me!" he said, chewing back a smile at her eagerness. He suspected that, like any beginner, she hadn't eaten breakfast.

Donna noticed that Adam was dressed for the city, in a business shirt and light trousers. He wasn't wearing a jacket, but these weren't his farm clothes, and his jet-black hair was slicked into place. He'd removed the last shred of the farm from his appearance.

She was suddenly very aware of her own disheveled state. Adam had already seen her faded old T-shirt, but at least she had been clean and tidy when she'd first seen him today. Now her hair was messed up and probably full of hayseeds, and of course he had to see her making a pig of herself.

She swallowed a large mouthful and said, "I didn't have time for breakfast this morning." Adam took up the chair beside her. She was sure she smelled of the barn.

"Not used to such early hours?" he asked mischievously. "You shouldn't stint on breakfast. It's your most important meal." As his eyes raked her tousled curls and glowing complexion, Adam thought she looked better for her morning's work. Her pallor had turned to a ruddy glow. "How did the first morning go, Donna?"

"Fine—I think?" she said, turning to Joe for confirmation.

"Yup, she's a natural," Joe grinned. "I was thinking, Adam, I might teach Donna to use the lawn tractor. We have a nice new one, the latest model," he said, turning to Donna. "The grass is getting pretty tall out front."

Adam nodded. "You should have worn a hat," he said to her. "The front lawn is mostly in the sun. I don't want you getting sunstroke. We'll find something in the house later." He noticed she had finished her muffin, and passed the plate.

"I'll make sure to have breakfast tomorrow," she said, and reached for another.

Adam and Joe talked about their work. Donna assumed from their conversation that Adam had been at the breeding farm. He mentioned that some colleagues, including a vet, would be coming to look over Rambo soon and decide his fate. There was one muffin left on the plate. Donna was still hungry, but she didn't want to take the last one, so she poured another cup of coffee instead, and put in plenty of cream.

After about a quarter of an hour, Joe said, "Time to get back to work. Are you all set, Donna?"

"I'll show Donna how to use the tractor," Adam said. "Maybe you'd bring it around for us, Joe?"

"Sure thing."

Joe left and Adam said, "Now we'll do something about that hat."

"I'm not really worried about freckles, but I guess I better protect myself."

He went into the kitchen and came out carrying a misshapen straw hat. The crown was dinted, and the brim sagged irregularly. Donna looked at it and laughed. She was afraid she might have earned another scowl, but Adam returned her smile. He set the hat on her head and tilted the brim rakishly over one eye. She was acutely conscious of his nearness. He didn't actually touch her, but putting the hat on seemed intimate. He kept looking at her while he arranged it, with that small smile curving his lips.

"You're all set for the Easter parade. Mom wears this for gardening," he said, stepping back to examine her. "It's nice and cool—lets the air circulate. You might remember that when you're buying your chapeau."

His flickering eyes took in her gold earrings. He was happy to see this one token of her former self. They added a certain something to her looks. "How do you like it so far?" he asked.

She found herself gazing into his smoky eyes, with the black curls of lashes, and forgetting what he had said. There was a strong aura of maleness about this man. Not just his size and looks, but in the way he moved, so sure of himself. "It feels fine," she said, "but I probably look like a hayseed."

"I wasn't talking about the hat. I meant the job. Joe likes you, but do you like us—the work, I mean?" he added rather too quickly when her eyes widened at the question.

"I like it fine, Adam." There was an air of restraint in her reply, due to the little misunderstanding.

"Good. Ah, here's Joe with the tractor." He picked up the last muffin and handed it to her. "You don't have to stand on ceremony here, Donna. I think you're still hungry."

"You're right," she said, and took a bite of it.

He inclined his head to hers and said, "And incidentally, the hat suits you."

She swallowed and gave him a sharp look. "Are you saying *I* look like a hick?"

"No, you make the hat look like the Boulevard Saint-Germain."

They went to join Joe at the shiny new tractor. He had pulled it up alongside her van. "Here she is. Isn't she a beauty!" he exclaimed. "I can show Donna how to run this thing, Adam. You don't want to get your good clothes dirty."

"That's all right," Adam said. "I'll do it."

Joe pressed on. "I'm not very busy...."

Adam gave a knowing smile. "You've had your chance, Joe. It's my turn."

Donna felt self-conscious with the men arguing over her company. She was also extremely curious to see what use Adam put his "turn" to. She thought he was embarrassed, because when he explained how to drive the tractor, he was all business.

"It has five gears. Other than that, it's really not very complicated for anyone who can drive a car. This is your car, I take it?" he said, glancing at the rusted rattletrap. Its condition was emphasized by the gleaming new paint of the yellow tractor. He was surprised that a Calvert wasn't driving something better.

"Only half mine," she said. "I share it with my cousin. Luckily Jeanie gets a car with her job, so I have the use of this for the present."

"The only danger in driving the tractor is in overturning it," Adam said. "You'd better stick to third gear the first time. Don't attempt the incline at the front end of the lawn. The men do the finishing with a power mower. Just do the flat stretches. You have to overlap a little in your runs, or you'll end up with strips of grass that aren't cut. Try to keep the lines straight."

She hopped up on the seat, and he showed her how to turn the motor on and perform the necessary functions. "A piece of cake," she said jauntily, above the motor's roar.

"If the job runs past twelve, you can stay and finish it this afternoon," he said.

Adam was becoming curious about her background. She had obviously told the truth when she said she was only a poor relation of the Calverts. She wouldn't have that old heap of a car if she had any money. If that was the case, she needed all the work she could get, yet she didn't seem happy at the chance for overtime. "We'll provide a ploughman's lunch," he added, thinking it was hunger that caused her obvious reluctance.

"Oh, I have to get away by twelve, Adam," she said. It didn't seem the time to go into details, when she was hollering over the motor, but she had been hired for mornings only, so she didn't think he'd be annoyed. She had to leave at twelve in order to get home, showered, changed, have lunch and get to the supermarket by two. "I can finish it tomorrow if I don't finish today."

"Suit yourself," he said, not angrily, but rather curtly.

Adam went into the house to change into his work clothes, and Donna drove the tractor around to the front. It drove beautifully, probably because it was brand new, she figured. She enjoyed mowing the lawn. It was fun, sitting up so high, with nothing between her and the weather. It really gave her the feel of the earth and the elements: the sun beating on her shoulders, and the cooling breeze from the surrounding trees. A collie dog appeared from somewhere and accompanied her, pacing along beside her, barking in pure animal pleasure from time to time. She mowed the shadowed space under the trees first, and when she moved into the sunlight, she was thankful for the straw hat that let the air circulate around her head while still shading her eyes. That was thoughtful of Adam....

He seemed quite nice, now that she was getting to know him a little. He had complimented her on her not very illustrious performance with the calves earlier. She foresaw difficulties if he expected her to be available for afternoon work whenever it pleased him, however. She'd have to tell him she had another job.

When she was nearly finished, a sleek sedan drove down the graveled lane toward the house. Donna watched to see who got out. It was an older woman, wearing fashionable culottes and carrying a few parcels. Mrs. Challow? The woman waved before entering the house, and Donna waved back. The collie darted off to join the woman, and Donna continued mowing. She was nearly finished by noon, and decided she could afford ten more minutes to finish the job. She only had about two more trips across the lawn to make when the tractor stopped dead.

Oh Lord! I've broken Adam's nice new machine, was her first awful thought. She tried to get it started again, but it just sat there. She went off for help, hoping it was Joe she met, and not Adam. But it was Adam who was just coming out of the barn, changed back into his work clothes and hat.

"Something the matter, Donna?" he asked.

She licked her lips nervously. "I don't know. I didn't do anything to it, but the tractor just stopped dead. I'm sorry."

A frown drew his black brows together. "I'll have a look," he said and walked around to the front with her. He looked at the freshly mowed lawn. She had done a good job—no wavy lines from crooked driving, no tall spaces between.

He went to the tractor, glanced at the dials, unscrewed a cap and looked down the opening. "Looks like you're out of gas," he said.

"Oh, thank heavens!" she exclaimed. "I was afraid I'd broken your nice new mower. I never thought of checking the gas," she admitted, feeling a little foolish. "Where do I get more to fill it?"

She glanced at her watch. It was five after twelve. Adam noticed it and said, "I'll ask Joe to finish up here. You seemed eager to get away."

"It *is* after twelve. I was only hired for mornings," she pointed out.

"Don't worry, you'll be paid time and a half for overtime. But I won't keep you. I said you can leave now, Donna."

"I am in kind of a hurry," she said. Too much of a hurry to go in to the tale of her having another job. He'd probably start asking questions. "I'm glad the mower's all right. I'll be back at six-thirty tomorrow. Bye." She waved and ran around to the patio, tossed the straw hat on the table, and went to her van.

When she drove down the driveway, she noticed that Adam was finishing the mowing himself. He didn't look up to wave as she passed. It was an uncomfortable ending to her first morning's work, but overall she thought things had gone pretty well. It was certainly more interesting than clerking at the supermarket.

Chapter Three

"How did the first day go?" Jeanie asked when Donna came in from work that night. "You look beat. Pretty hard, huh?"

"Samara was fun, but the store was a madhouse. There's a tenth anniversary sale going on, and one of the cashiers phoned in sick. We had customers lined up waiting for carts. All coffee breaks were cut short. I'm beat." Donna flopped into a chair and drew a weary sigh.

"I made supper, so you can just take it easy and tell me all about Adam Challow," Jeanie said. "What is he?"

Donna knew her cousin wasn't asking Adam's profession, but his astrological sign. "I don't know. We didn't discuss signs. Acts like a Leo, though. King of all he surveys. A natural leader."

"Ardent, sincere—affectionate?" Jeanie asked, with a grin.

"Give me time. I hardly know the man!"

"Why don't you ask him out?" Donna stared at Jeanie in disbelief. "What's wrong with that? It's the nineties. You never take the initiative. I would, if it were me."

"Well, it's not you. It's me. What are we eating?" she asked, to finish this subject.

"Salad and deviled eggs."

They discussed their day's work as they ate. Jeanie had met a new man when she was selling advertising at the local sports shop. She had a date with him that night. Donna didn't ask who had invited whom out. She felt that she was a bit too slow, but she had no desire to equal Jeanie's Olympic speed at getting dates.

Donna stayed home to study her book on screenwriting. She wanted to be ready to talk to Matt Hibbert when he came the next week. She was bone-tired from her two jobs and went to bed early to be ready for another hard day. She set the clock half an hour earlier to allow time for breakfast, and left her boots outside the front door.

Work became easier over the remainder of the week as she learned her way around Samara. Her biological clock adjusted to the new schedule of early to bed and early to rise. Unused muscles hardened to their task, and she felt stronger for it. In the evening, she managed a few hours to study the book on screenwriting.

Instead of buying a straw hat for work, she wore a peaked baseball cap that was just as effective against the sun. Mac Davis, the sports store owner Jeanie was seeing, had given her half a dozen of them as a promotion. The one Donna chose was a hot neon pink.

She spent a fair bit of time with Joe, learning the business. He was easy to talk to, and she was soon confiding all her writing plans to him. She also met Mrs. Challow at the morning coffee breaks. Adam's mother had been in America so long that she had lost her French accent, but she oc-

casionally used French phrases. She had also maintained her
Gallic vivacity and zest for life. When she joined them for
coffee, the air rang with laughter. Donna was a little intimidated by her and did more listening than talking.

Donna still had no luck finding work boots to fit, but be-
cause a fully grown cow had stepped on her toe, turning it
black and blue, she planned to drive into Watertown that
Saturday and not come home until she had found a pair.
Before spending the money, however, she meant to ask
Adam whether she had passed her probation.

They met often during the week, and although he hadn't
complained, she had made a few mistakes due to inexperi-
ence. Once or twice he had assigned her a job, then changed
his mind. "I'd better get one of the men to do that," he had
said when they were putting the hay in. The way he looked
at her at these times kept her fully aware that she was a
woman and he was a man. It was something in his eyes. . . .
She never got the feeling that he wished she were a man,
even though some of the work was really too heavy for a
woman.

Before leaving Friday at noon, she went in search of
Adam. She knew he was around the farm, because his station wagon was in the driveway. She had learned that he
spent a good deal of time in his office, but she hadn't been
into that part of the house yet.

There was a surprising amount of office work in running
a large farm. He had to keep his financial accounts, he cor-
responded with a wide circle of professional colleagues, and
he also kept breeding records with individual files on the
yield of each cow.

She found him bent over a computer, tapping in information. If she hadn't known he was a farmer, she would
have believed him to be a busy executive. He seemed equally
at home in either role. His broad shoulders and wiry

strength suited the physical side of his job, but there was obviously an acute brain inside his head.

Sunlight streamed into the oak-lined office, highlighting Adam's lean cheeks and carved profile. Donna sensed a pent-up energy in his air of concentration. Oak seemed the proper material to surround him. He was strong as oak, and rather unbending.

Adam looked up and smiled. He had unconsciously formed the habit of looking from the corner of his eyes for that neon pink cap as he went about his work. He told himself he was always concerned about a new employee, but that couldn't account for his sudden eagerness for the morning coffee breaks, when they could relax together.

It was hard to believe that this woman who looked like an urchin with a dirty face was the same elegant creature who had come to him a week ago in an immaculate shirt and riding breeches.

He knew by now that she wasn't afraid of hard work. He blamed his French side for preferring the more elegant woman, but either of her sides could make his blood pump faster.

"What a lovely office!" she exclaimed.

"Why, thank you. But I can't take the credit for it. I inherited it from my father."

Her eyes made a slow tour of the paneled walls. One was lined with bookcases, another held three colorful paintings, framed in ornate gilt. She didn't recognize the artists, although she thought they were post-impressionists.

"You're not a Libra, are you?" she asked.

"I beg your pardon?"

"Your sign. Are you a Libra? Libras are artistic." She indicated the paintings.

"I was born on Christmas Eve. I believe that makes me a Capricorn, but whether it makes me artistic I leave to the experts. I haven't seen any evidence of it myself."

"You're a Capricorn!" she exclaimed, frowning. Jeanie didn't care much for Capricorns. They were said to be headstrong and unyielding. Natural fighters, strong will-power. In a word, stubborn.

Adam apparently wasn't interested in astrology. "My mother bought these paintings in Paris some years ago. She firmly believes the bridge scene is a Renoir. We don't disillusion her. What can I do for you, Donna?" he asked, motioning to a chair.

She sat on the edge of it, as if ready for flight. "The week's up. We agreed to a week's trial period. I came to—"

"You're not leaving!" he exclaimed, rising up from his chair in alarm. His heart lurched in his chest.

She blinked in surprise. "Not unless you want me to. I love it here."

His heart settled down to a constant thud. "You're doing a great job."

She beamed at the unexpected compliment. "Thanks, Adam. I'll go out and buy my work boots, then. I didn't want to spend my hard-earned money on them until I knew whether I'd be staying."

"Joe mentioned you couldn't find a pair in Bayville." His smoky eyes examined her in a way that made her very aware of her femininity. "I was over in Watertown yesterday. I got you something." He reached down behind his desk and lifted a large box, which he handed to her.

"Thank you," she said, bewildered. What could it be? That slow smile suggested something personal. She lifted the lid and saw a small pair of work boots. A nervous laugh escaped from her throat. That Adam was giving her any present was a shock. She hardly knew what to expect, but she certainly did not expect a pair of boots. It occurred to her that he hadn't actually used the word present. He probably expected her to pay for them.

"Try them on," he said.

"You mean here, now?"

"If they're not right they'll have to be exchanged. I had to guess at your size, although I had a pretty good idea—" He came to a sudden stop. She didn't look at him, but it occurred to her that he must have been watching her pretty closely. "I got them in the boy's department. I'm going into Watertown this afternoon. I can change them today if they don't fit."

She took off her winter boots and slid on the metal-toed boots while Adam watched. He left his chair and perched on the edge of his desk to see her better. They seemed to fit just right, but when she tried to walk, she felt as if she had on lead weights. The boots clumped awkwardly when she took a few steps and made her feel clumsy. She held her arms out in front of her. "I feel like Frankenstein's monster," she said, laughing.

"You don't look like him," Adam replied.

She was suddenly very aware of her disheveled appearance. Adam wasn't dressed in his working clothes today. His office was very elegant, making her feel out of place, and unattractive. But if he found her unattractive, he did a good job of hiding it. That warm smile and the light in his gray eyes suggested admiration.

She took a few steps and sat down again. "The fit is fine. How much did they cost, Adam? I'll have to pay you on Monday."

"They're a present," he said.

"You don't have to do that." In fact, she wished he hadn't. She felt uncomfortable accepting a gift from him.

"Employers usually supply equipment for the job, don't they? I don't believe firemen or policemen have to buy their uniforms. Why should you?"

"The other hands here buy their own things, though," she said, looking at him in question.

"I pay them more than minimum wage. In fact, now that your probationary period is over, we'll do something about your salary."

This pleased her more than the boots, and a smile peeped out. She did feel that such hard work deserved something more than minimum wage. Even the supermarket paid a little more than that. "Good! I can sure use it."

He mentioned her new salary, but as a businessman himself, Adam knew that even with the increase, it still wasn't enough to provide a decent living. He had overcome any idea that she was wealthy. Her staying on at this job would have told him, even if her well-used van hadn't.

"I'm afraid you must have a tough time making ends meet, Donna," he said. "I'll see if I can extend your hours."

He was *pitying* her! Her pride flared at this speech. She didn't want pity! Giving her the boots was a thoughtful gesture, especially as the pay was not very good, but she had no intention of accepting charity. "Actually I'm pretty busy," she said stiffly.

"Too busy to work a couple of afternoons a week?" he asked. His expression told her he thought he was being her fairy godfather, doing her a big favor. "Time and a half. In fact, you can start today, if that's convenient."

"I'm afraid I couldn't manage that, Adam."

His brows drew together in a sharp frown. She had been planning to tell him about her other job, and this seemed like the right time for it, but she decided against it. He'd only go into his pitying mode again.

"Just today, or are all your afternoons taken up?" he asked. She didn't like that sniffy tone, as if it was his God-given right to have her work whenever it suited him.

"I'm busy in the afternoons." Should she tell him? She drew her bottom lip between her teeth in indecision.

Adam found himself at a loss. She was short of money, but wasn't willing to work whole days. These modern kids!

No ambition. They'd rather live in a hovel than do an honest day's work. She probably spent her afternoons hanging out at the beach.

"Suit yourself," he said. He rose and added in an injured tone, "You *will* be back Monday?"

Donna bent over to remove the boots. "I'll be here," she said through clenched teeth.

"It's nearly noon. You'll be anxious to be leaving. Don't let me keep you." He returned to his computer and ignored her.

Donna stuffed the boots into the box. "Thanks for the boots," she said.

"You're welcome. Be sure you wear them. I don't want any expensive accidents."

Expensive accidents! That's all he was worried about—having to pay compensation. She was fuming by the time she reached her van. This whole boot thing was an exercise in poor taste, as if she didn't know enough to buy a pair herself. It was a grotesque parody of the Cinderella story. Metal-toed boots instead of a glass slipper. Adam was sure no Prince Charming.

She drove home, showered and changed, ate lunch and hurried over to the supermarket to put in another four hours.

Back at Samara, Mrs. Challow went to her son's office when she heard Donna's van cough into motion. Her flashing brown eyes glared at her son.

"You were supposed to ask Donna to stay to lunch," she said. "What happened?"

"She had other plans, Mom."

"I made my special *coquilles Saint-Jacques*. You'll have to eat two helpings. Ask her on Monday, then. That child is too thin."

"Donna is not a child."

"You said something to offend her," Mrs. Challow said. With a shake of her head, she left.

Adam sat on alone, thinking about it. His mother was an incorrigible matchmaker. Her French soul could not comprehend that he was still single at thirty. "A farmer needs a wife," she often told him. "I'm too old to run this house. I want you to build me a little cottage with no stairs for my retirement. Right on the corner of our property, so I can see all the traffic on the road."

It was inevitable that his mother should light on Donna as a likely prospect. She put forward any stray woman who came into their midst. The neighbors, business contacts, women she met in Bayville or at church—she wanted them all, one after the other, as her daughter-in-law. Usually Adam made a joke out of it, but with Donna, he felt differently.

He wasn't in love—he hardly knew her—but he wanted to know her better. There was some vital chemistry between them, waiting to be explored. His pulse always raced when she was near, and he sensed that she was very aware of him, too. An aura of sexual attraction flared whenever they were together.

Without that necessary ingredient, he couldn't be interested in any woman. There was that much of his mother's romantic nature in him that he had to feel a physical attraction before he pursued a woman.

But even with that attraction, she was wrong for him. She was a drifter. Not interested in getting ahead. She probably wanted a good time out of life and was willing to pick up odd jobs when necessary. One day she'd walk into his office and say offhandedly, "Oh, by the way, I'll be moving on next week." No point getting involved with a woman like that. He shut off his computer and joined his mother for lunch.

"I'm making a chocolate torte for the church bake sale tomorrow, Adam," Mrs. Challow said. "I need baking chocolate. You're going to the breeding farm this afternoon?"

"Yes, I have to arrange for Rambo to be picked up on Monday. We've decided to take him to the co-op farm. You want me to get the chocolate?"

"And a dozen eggs. I should never have given up my chickens. The eggs from the supermarket—bah! They are not fresh. But I am too old to keep chickens."

"If you're definitely through with that project, I'll tear down the chicken coop and turn it into a garage."

Mrs. Challow lifted her flashing eyes from the *coquilles Saint-Jacques*. "Your wife might want to raise chickens," she said firmly. "It was the custom in my country."

"I didn't realise the good wives of Paris reared chickens."

"Naturally I am speaking of my relatives in the country."

It was five-thirty when Adam left the breeders' farm and drove into Bayville. They had received a lucrative order for sperm from their bank, and he was in a good mood. The day was sultry. He was looking forward to a dip in the pool before dinner. He nearly forgot his mother's shopping, but as he passed the Bayville supermarket, he was reminded by an advertisement for a special on eggs.

He wandered through the busy aisles, jostled by carts and shoppers and feeling out of place, until he found the baking chocolate. He got two packages and some walnuts, hoping to coerce his mother into baking brownies, as well. She considered brownies a barbaric sweet. Her own taste was for exotic French desserts, heavy with whipped cream and liqueurs, and puff pastry. After more searching, he found the dairy department and got the eggs.

There was a lineup at the four checkout counters, but a kindly woman steered him to the express line.

The cashiers all wore little peaked pink-and-white caps and pink uniforms. The cap reminded him of Donna. A young mother with a howling youngster in front of him distracted his attention. The child was trying to climb out of the seat, and Adam helped her restrain him. He didn't glance at the cashier until he placed his groceries on the counter.

When he glanced up, he could scarcely believe his eyes. He noticed right away that she looked bored and tired. It was like seeing a racehorse pulling a wagon, and it angered him. "Donna! What are you doing here?" he exclaimed. It occurred to him that she had found another job. That she wasn't planning to come back to Samara. She *had* seemed angry about something when she left.

Donna was annoyed at being found out. He must think it strange that she hadn't told him. She drew the chocolate over the machine that read the code bar. "What does it look like?" she asked irritably. She priced the walnuts. The eggs weren't coded. She punched in the price, and the bill was issued from the machine. "That'll be six sixty-five, Adam."

"You work here?" he asked, his mind in confusion. Her speedy motions told him this wasn't her first day. She moved so quickly her hands were a blur.

"Afternoons only. I told you I was busy in the afternoons."

"But I thought—"

She glanced at the long line and repeated, "That'll be six sixty-five," as she bagged his few purchases.

He drew out a ten dollar bill and handed it to her. She made change and handed it back. "Have a nice day," she said, in the insincere, singsong voice of long repetition.

Adam took his bag, but didn't want to leave. He felt in some way that it was his fault she had to work here, doing this dull, repetitious job. "When are you finished?" he asked.

The next customer had already slid her purchases forward and was waiting to be served.

"Six o'clock," Donna said.

A basket was bumped against his legs, not quite by accident, he thought. "Are you through?" the next customer asked him.

"Yes. Sorry." He took his bag and left the counter.

It was a quarter to six. Only fifteen minutes... He got himself a can of cola from the machine near the door and sipped it. Glancing at her counter, he could see how busy she was and felt a rush of pity. Poor kid. He had certainly misjudged her. Why the devil hadn't she told him she had another job? It must be as boring as hell, and hard, too, standing on her feet all afternoon after working all morning.

Donna frowned in exasperation as she finished her shift. Why hadn't she told Adam? She didn't want him pitying her. She told herself she hoped he wasn't waiting for her, yet when she allowed herself one quick look for him, she was disappointed that she didn't see him. It wasn't until her replacement came on that she spotted Adam.

The employees' lounge was in the opposite direction, toward the back of the store. She didn't have to pass Adam to reach it. She changed quickly out of her uniform into a skirt and blouse, wondering if he was still there. At the mirror she fluffed out her hair and applied a daub of lipstick. Her color was good after her job at Samara, but she felt like a dishrag.

She tried to look nonchalant as she went toward the door. She managed a well-simulated look of surprise when she met him, although she had spotted him a minute before.

"Adam. Are you waiting for me?" she asked.

"I thought I'd give you a lift home—or do you have your van?"

"I don't waste gas driving to work in the good weather, but you didn't have to wait. I only live a few blocks from here."

"I'll drive you. I'd like to talk." He noticed that mention of not wasting gas.

Adam dropped his can in the recycling bin, and they went in search of his station wagon. He unlocked the door and they got in. She thought they might talk in the wagon, but Adam left the parking lot without even asking where she lived.

"I live on the corner of Elm and Radcliffe," she said. "You can turn left on Maine."

"I know where it is."

He drove directly there, still without saying what he wanted to talk about, although she had a pretty good idea. He pulled up to the apartment doorway and stopped.

Adam turned and gazed at her. "Why didn't you tell me you had an afternoon job, Donna?" he asked. The curiosity in his voice was tinged with both pity and injury.

"It didn't come up."

"It should have, when I asked you to work some afternoons. Why didn't you tell me? What's the secret?"

Guilt lent her reply a sharp edge. She lifted her chin and said, "I didn't want you to feel sorry for me. And don't say you didn't, because you did. Why else did you buy me those boots?"

Adam continued gazing at her. "You were too proud to admit it," he said. "Not that there's anything wrong with it. It's admirable. Not many youngsters nowadays—"

"I'm not a youngster! And all the people my age that I know work their buns off. I don't know where you old—older people get off intimating we're lazy."

"I don't know many people your age," he admitted. "The fellows I've hired don't seem to take their work very seriously. They come and go."

"Why should they kill themselves to make you rich? Being a farmhand is hardly a life's career. If they get a chance to better themselves, why shouldn't they take it?"

"There's a grain of truth in that. I do hire mostly casual labor for seasonal work. It's hard to get good farm help, but I treat my employees fairly. I can't say they always reciprocate."

"That wasn't a personal complaint. I don't feel I've been badly treated in any way. Thanks for the lift, Adam. I imagine you want to get home."

"Wait." His hand came out and caught her wrist. It was the first time Adam had touched her. His fingers felt warmly possessive. A tingle like a mild electric shock ran up her arm. "I wanted to say something else." She just looked at him, waiting. "I'm sorry for this afternoon. I'm afraid I was a little out of line," he said gently.

"That's all right."

"Friends?" His hand slid down to her fingers and gave them a friendly squeeze.

"Sure. Let's not make a federal case out of it. I'll see you Monday morning—in my Frankenstein boots," she added, trying for a light touch.

"Monday's a long way off. Why don't you see me tonight—in your dancing slippers?"

"You mean for a date?" she asked, blinking in surprise. Her first reaction was a thrill of excitement, but it soon ebbed to uncertainty. Dating the boss didn't seem like a very good idea.

"Boy calls for girl, takes her out to dinner and dancing. Yes, I guess you could call it a date."

"Gee, I don't—" Two things happened at the same time. Donna noticed that Adam's eyes darkened in what looked very much like disappointment. The other was that she realized she wanted to be with him away from the farm, where she could get to know him better.

"That was selfish of me," Adam said. It was her turn to look disappointed. "You won't want to dance after being on your feet all day."

She was a little peeved that he gave up so easily. "Actually I have plans for dinner." The plan was just to meet Jeanie at the corner fast food restaurant, but it was too late to cancel. It would be selfish to leave Jeanie waiting, although she'd be furious if Donna turned Adam down. Maybe she could call the restaurant and leave a message....

"Then you already have a date," Adam said. "I should have realized—the weekend, after all. Are you seriously involved with someone?"

"I'm very much involved—with my cousin Jeanie. You're welcome to join us for a hamburger if you like," she suggested as an alternative. Jeanie was discreet. She wouldn't hang on after dinner. "Strictly casual."

"Three's a crowd," he said, but he looked interested.

When Donna mentioned that they were to meet in half an hour, he had to refuse. It didn't leave him time to get home and change. "We might still be able to rescue something of the evening. I could be back here by eight," he said, cocking an eyebrow to see if she was interested.

A smile began in her eyes and slowly spread to her lips. "You're a Capricorn, all right. They're good at overcoming obstacles."

"I expect that's a euphemism for stubborn. I'm glad we're good for something. What other characteristics do we possess?"

"You have the reputation of going to any excess to carry out your plans."

He tilted his head, considering this idea. "You'd better say yes, then, to spare me from kidnapping you."

"What the heck. I'm a Gemini. We're versatile—changeable in our views."

"Don't change your mind about this. I'll be here at eight. See you then."

He got out and opened her door. Donna waved and ran into the apartment, smiling.

Chapter Four

"This is a new record for you, Donna," Jeanie joked. "You've only known Adam a week and you've got a date already."

"I don't aspire to match your record," Donna said. The hamburgers and fries had arrived. The weekend was just beginning, and they were both in a mood to celebrate with a few laughs.

"That'd be Larry, from college. He didn't even say hello. He just walked by, winked at me, I smiled, and he said, 'Hi, would you like to go for a coffee?' About a minute. Yeah, that's my record."

"You can do better. Men have run a quarter of a mile in a minute, Jeanie. Go for thirty seconds."

"I'm working on it. So what are you going to wear tonight?"

"I suggested casual," Donna said, spearing a potato and dipping it in ketchup.

"What are you going to do? Are you going to a movie, or what?"

"I don't know, Jeanie. We're just going out on a casual date."

"This is not casual. It's chaos. What if you wear jeans and he comes in a suit?"

"Then he'll laugh me to scorn, tell me he never wants to see my face at Samara again, and leave. Maybe the world will come to an end, as well. It'll be all right. He won't wear a suit. And I don't intend to wear jeans. Don't worry about it."

"You're right. I worry too much. It's a Taurus failing. But we're kind and generous. I was just thinking, Donna, Capricorn is an earth sign. You're air. They don't harmonize."

"We weren't planning to sing any duets." Jeanie wasn't satisfied with a joke where horoscopes were concerned. "The air and earth have coexisted a few millenia without disaster," she added.

"You don't call our environment a disaster? Sometimes I think you don't take all this seriously enough, Donna. A Capricorn isn't right for you. They're dogged; you Geminis are fickle."

"I am not fickle!"

"Well, you like change. If he falls in love with you and you meet somebody else, there's no saying what he'll do. Capricorns will go to great extremes to get what they want."

"I know. Adam mentioned kidnapping me if I refused," Donna said, to goad her friend.

"All right, laugh. Just don't say I didn't warn you."

They ate for a moment in silence, then Jeanie said, "You could ask Adam to Uncle Mike's party. It's going to be a really big event. He's hired an orchestra and everything."

"That's not until a week from tomorrow night. I'll wait and see how things work out."

They went back to the apartment as soon as they were finished. Even a casual date with a man like Adam Challow required lavish preparations.

After trying three different outfits, Donna settled on a sarong skirt that draped across the front and tied at the front. It emphasized her slender waist and shapely hips, and added a note of flirtation. As the skirt was a plain beige, she chose a jungle-patterned sleeveless top to brighten it up. Her hair was always a little unmanageable in the humidity of summer, but its curly abandon suited the outfit. Her heightened color suited it, too. With her gold hoop earrings, she looked a little like a Gypsy.

When the doorbell rang at eight sharp, Jeanie said, "The place is a mess! Why don't you go upstairs and meet him in the lobby?"

Donna glanced around and realized that the apartment was looking pretty ragged. It was impossible to make a basement apartment elegant, but that night it wasn't even tidy. Newspapers were spread over the coffee table. The kitchen, which was visible from the living room, still held the morning dishes. They usually only did the dishes after dinner, as they were in a mad rush in the morning. With a fleeting memory of Adam's lovely house, she agreed.

"Have a good time," Jeanie called.

"I intend to." Donna grinned and ran upstairs to meet Adam. The lobby was decorated to lend a touch of class to the building. It had dark marble floors and lighter marble walls, interspersed with panels of gold silk. A chandelier and a few large plants completed the decor.

"This is very nice," Adam said, looking around after they had exchanged greetings. He was a little surprised at the opulent marble, considering Donna had mentioned she was short of money.

"Mike rents it to us at a special price," she explained.

She was relieved to see he was wearing a casual sports shirt, khaki trousers and sneakers.

Adam just stood a moment, gazing at her. This was more or less how he had first seen Donna. The clothes were different, of course, but the overall effect was the same. She looked glamorous and beautiful, in a way that no woman could look when she was working around a farm. She was even wearing the same gold earrings and that little diamond bracelet.

"If this is casual, I'd like to see you when you're all dressed up," he said. His smoky eyes lingered on her face, made a quick flickering assessment of her body, then returned to settle on her eyes. "Shall we go?"

He held the door, and they went out to his station wagon.

"Where *are* we going?" she asked.

"I thought we'd do something easy after your hard day."

"A movie?" she asked, a little disappointed. You didn't get much chance to get to know a person sitting in a movie theater.

Adam looked around at the tree-lined street and up at the sky. It was a twilight blue, streaked with peach and saffron as the sun sank behind tall buildings. Swallows and blackbirds swooped overhead, singing their pleasure. "It's such a lovely night it seems a shame to waste it locked up in a theater. Was there something special you wanted to see?" he asked.

"No, I was hoping you didn't want to go to a movie, actually. I just don't know what there is to do in Bayville."

He opened the wagon door and she slid inside. Adam joined her. "I keep a little boat down at the marina. It would be a nice evening to be on the water. Would you like to go for a spin?"

"I'd love it!" she exclaimed.

The local marina was only a few blocks away. On this sultry July evening many tired workers had the same idea of escaping the heat by taking a run along the shore. Adam spoke to a few people, but didn't stop to introduce Donna. He went directly to a boat and began untying it.

"A little boat" seemed the wrong description for the sleek inboard motorboat that would hold six without crowding. Its varnished hull shone in the rays of the setting sun. Chrome gleamed along the edges and on the dashboard. The bucket seats were upholstered in dark leather and were as comfortable as a sofa.

Adam turned the key, and they pulled away from the dock at a slow pace, as there was considerable boat traffic. Once they were on the open river, he let out the throttle and the boat shot forward. The prow sliced into the water like a knife and left a roiling wake of foam behind. There was a glass windshield, but the wind flew over the top of it, pulling Donna's hair back from her face.

"There's a scarf in the glove compartment if you want it," Adam said. He had to raise his voice over the sound of the motor.

Talking was difficult so Donna shook her head. The whipping wind was cool and refreshing. This ride was the perfect ending to a hectic, tiring day. All she had to do was sit and enjoy it. The city shoreline was commercial, but as they drove west, the shoreline became greener and prettier. The cottages tucked in among tall trees looked like picture-postcards. People on the docks waved, and Donna waved back. It was hard to believe these were probably the same people who gave her a hard time at the store. What was it about the river that made everyone mellow? Or was it that the hassle of city living turned nice people cranky?

Donna had a perfect view of the sunset. She watched, mesmerized, as the gleaming red ball melted into the river. The sky around it was like a kaleidoscope in slow motion, but a kaleidoscope that showed no jagged edges. Scarlet and copper and orange shifted and reflected from puffs of cloud, all streaked with gold needles from the dying rays of the sun.

Adam cut back on the throttle, and the roaring motor dulled to a hum. "Isn't it beautiful," she said, drawing a deep, luxurious sigh.

"It kind of makes it all worthwhile," Adam said.

She turned in surprise. "All what? You have a pretty good life, Adam. That prosperous farm!"

"As you may have read from the newspapers, farmers are in a lot of financial trouble these days. A farm doesn't become prosperous without a lot of hard work and ingenuity. Having livestock is like having a whole houseful of children. They can't manage on their own. Dairy products aren't in as high demand as they used to be, either, with everyone worrying about animal fat."

"You seem to be doing very well."

"As I said, it takes a lot of hard work—and some understanding employees," he added, to show her he appreciated her.

"You could always leave Joe in charge if you wanted to get away for a while," she pointed out.

"I do, sometimes. Joe is a great help. I want to get him into the breeding co-op with me. There's good money to be made there. Europe and even Asia are interested in our holsteins. They're the best milk producers in the world; sometimes they produce more than we can sell. Thank God for the man who discovered the science of dehydrating milk."

After they had enjoyed a lengthy drive, he turned the wheel and the boat veered toward an island. "This is Elbow Island State Park," he said. "There are picnic tables and barbecue pits here. Also a dock. You can see by the shape of it how the island got its name."

A layered outcropping of limestone was shaped roughly like a man's bent arm. Fir trees and bushes grew on top of the stone, like icing on a cake. Adam steered the boat into the bay made by the crook in the elbow and pulled in at the dock. There were three other boats there, and two children played in the shallow water on one side where sand had been dumped to form a wading beach.

"It's getting a little dark for it tonight, but we'll come here some afternoon and have a picnic," Adam said. "It's a nice place to explore. Just big enough to get lost, without having to worry that you'll never find your way out."

Donna felt a thrill of satisfaction at the assumption that they'd be going out together in the future. "Life is fun when you're rich enough to have a boat," she said.

"Yeah, if making your money leaves you time to enjoy it. This is only the second time I've been out this year."

He got up and helped Donna onto the dock. "We should have brought something to toast. Marshmallows or something," she said. Two family groups were cooking hamburgers on the grills.

"I have a bottle of wine in the boat. Next time I'll bring marshmallows."

Adam got the wine and two glasses. They went to a table perched on top of a little cliff, away from the picnickers. Below them, the river rippled calmly, burnished to copper by the sinking sun. One of the families had lit a bonfire on the shore and were beginning to sing folk songs. It lent a nostalgic touch to the outing.

Adam poured the wine and handed Donna a glass. "Cheers," she said, touching her glass to his.

They fell into an easy, relaxed mood, with the sky darkening above them and a breeze whispering in the trees behind. A fat white moon hung low in the sky, casting a net of light on the water. In the sky a wilderness of stars twinkled, promising good weather ahead.

"Where are you from, Donna?" Adam asked. It was the first time they had been alone for any length of time, and he was curious to discover her past.

"I'm from Buffalo. I haven't roamed very far from home."

"Any particular reason why you chose Bayville?"

She told him about attending college with Jeanie, and how Jeanie got a job on their uncle's newspaper.

Adam listened, not surprised that she had a good education, but surprised that she was putting it to such little use. "I can understand your cousin coming here, but what about you? There aren't many opportunities for a Lit. major in Bayville."

"I want to write," she said, feeling rather foolish confessing it. "I can do that anyplace. I don't intend to stand behind a counter all my life, you know. The store and the farm are just to pay the bills until I can support myself with my writing."

"So that explains it. I wondered about a Calvert being so unambitious."

"But I'm very ambitious! One day I'll write a bestseller, but right now I haven't lived enough. You have to experience life firsthand before you can write anything meaningful. So I'm starting with short stories and articles. Practicing my craft."

Her eyes sparkled when she talked about her work. Her whole face became animated. The breeze flirted through her curls, adding to her sense of animation. Adam had often seen her angry and determined, but this was a side he hadn't suspected, and he warmed to her.

"What sort of thing do you write?" he asked.

"Things with a woman's slant, for women's magazines." She mentioned some of the large ones and told him how hard it was to break in.

He listened with interest. "I understand writing's a competitive business. You might try the smaller trade magazines. The dairy farmers have their own periodical. It only comes out bimonthly, but they do articles and fiction. Even a little poetry. And the pay's not bad."

"What could I tell a dairy farmer?" she asked. "I'm a complete beginner. Writers should write about what they know. That's why I don't mind getting experience at all sorts of jobs."

"I wasn't suggesting anything in the 'how-to' line. But an outsider's look at the perils and pleasures might be interesting."

"It's a pretty good idea," she said.

They finished one glass of wine, and Adam poured another. Fireflies appeared in the bushes, adding a touch of magic. "I'm sorry I was difficult about your working some afternoons," he said. "I admire your ambition, and your working so hard to achieve your goals."

"You don't need me full-time, and I can't afford to toss up my other job. But I could use the extra money. I'm saving for a word processor. It'd save so much time. Maybe I could work Saturdays if anything came up that needed another hand."

"We'll work something out. And if you need time off—if you get an assignment and need extra time to work on it—we're flexible at the farm. Just let me know the day before. Some of the local farmers have sons who are always glad to get extra work in the summer. They work at home, of course, but they're happy to pick up a few extra dollars on the side."

"That's very considerate of you, Adam." Suspiciously considerate. She thought of the boots and added, "I hope you're not just taking pity on me."

He set down his glass and gazed at her. A slow smile curved his lips. "It's not pity. I'm more devious than that. I like having you around."

"What for, comic relief?" she asked.

"Wrong again," he said, and seized her hand. "Would you like to try again?"

Darkness shadowed his face, but the husky burr of his voice gave a hint of his meaning. Before she could think of an answer, he inclined his head to hers, and she felt a soft brush against her cheek. A heady scent of pine was in the air, and the stars twinkled mischievously above.

If ever a night had been made for romance, this was surely it. A gentle breeze moved her hair, but it wasn't the breeze that made her quiver. It was the intimate touch of Adam's lips on her cheek, moving now down to the hollow of her throat in a sensuous glide that made her scalp tingle. In about three seconds he was going to kiss her, and she wasn't sure she was ready for that.

She shimmied down the bench and said in a quaking voice that betrayed her uncertainty, "It must be getting late. We should go now."

He put his arm around her and pulled her back. His lips brushed against her throat as he answered, "Look at the time! It must be nine o'clock!" A chuckle rumbled from his chest, as both arms closed around her.

Then he raised his head. Not four inches above her, his eyes gleamed silver in the moonlight, and a soft sigh escaped her. He was coming closer, his face blurring, until all she could see was his lips. They trembled slightly as they settled on hers for a deep kiss that shook her to her very foundations.

Adam had always sensed that this fiery chemistry was there, hovering like a candle flame between them, but he hadn't realized it would flare into passion so quickly. He wanted to feel her soft warmth, and drew her close against him. It was even better than he had hoped. The feminine thrust of her breasts gave an exciting resistance before melting against the wall of his chest.

He wanted to feel her all over, and moved one hand to touch her face. It brushed as lightly as a bird's wing over her brow, before cupping her cheek and chin in a possessive grip. At the same time, his lips moved hungrily. His other hand went as if by instinct to her breast and held it in his palm.

Donna felt the heat rising and was afraid what might come next. She put her hand on his to move it away, but found she was reluctant to do it. His fingers moved slowly, gently squeezing, while his lips persuaded her to accept. It was a strangely hypnotic sensation, almost as though she had no will in the matter. It felt dangerously exciting, but it felt right, too.

It was not until she felt a moist flicker at her lips that she became alarmed. This was all happening too fast! She still had to work for Adam and didn't want this kiss to get out of control. She tried to slide away. His arms drew her back effortlessly. She tried again, and felt herself lurch. She was falling off the bench.

They both laughed as they realized what was happening. It provided a necessary check to their rising passion. "I'm afraid I got a little carried away," Adam said.

"Let's blame it on the romantic setting," she said. Her voice was breathless and pulsing.

Adam kissed her nose. "Sure, Donna. It was all the moon's fault. What excuse will we use when it happens on the farm?"

"It won't happen at the farm. There I'll have to remember you're my boss."

"Suppose I make Joe your boss," he said, laughing at the transparency of this ruse.

"Seriously, Adam. I don't think it's a good idea for us to—you know—have a relationship when I'm working for you."

"What do I have to do, fire you?"

"No, you just have to control yourself. And so do I. Let's go."

They went back to the boat and returned to town. Night on the river was completely different from daytime. Black water shimmered mysteriously around them as they flew together through the darkness. The shoreline had become a wonderland of colored lights. She hadn't realized Bayville was so big. It stretched, seemingly for miles, like a large city. It occurred to her that it was like the difference between liking someone and loving them. In daylight, you see everything, warts and all, when you are with a friend. But at night you were blinded to everything but the glitter of the "lights," as lovemaking blinds you to a person's faults.

"Is it too early for something to eat?" Adam asked, interrupting her line of thought.

"Are you kidding? It's been hours since I had that measly hamburger. And a measly large chips and chocolate milk," she added. "Only about a zillion calories. But I didn't have any dessert."

"Then we'll have some dessert. How does a sundae sound to you?"

"We could have double-decker ice-cream cones. Good for the dairy business," she pointed out.

"You've talked me into it."

Adam drove to the drive-in and ordered the ice-cream cones. They ate them in the car, parked between other cars. The lights of the drive-in created an aura of daytime. The glamour of night had receded, and she tried to enjoy Adam as a friend.

"I haven't done this since high school," Adam admitted with a boyish grin.

"Jeanie and I often come here. Where do you usually take your dates?"

"Out for dinner or dancing. Since you're working two jobs, I'll have to get you home early during the week."

"I didn't say I'd go out with you again," she replied, but her smile showed her interest in the idea.

"True. And I didn't ask you," he parried.

"You implied you would."

"You didn't object when I implied the same thing on the island. We agreed to go there during the day and explore."

"I didn't agree. I just didn't disagree. I was neutral. You're taking me for granted."

"I'm a Capricorn. Blame it on the stars."

"Why not? We've already blamed the other thing on the moon."

"Other thing?" he asked, feigning offense. "That's a cavalier way to refer to our first kiss."

"I mentally gave it capitals," she said.

"Hmm, I don't think I've ever embraced a woman in capitals before. I like it. I can hardly wait till we get to italics."

The conversation was so ridiculous she hardly knew what to say, but his tone gave a hint of double entendre. "I don't want you talking dirty to me, Adam," she said, laughing.

"Huh! Who's the one who gave Our Thing capitals in the first place?"

"Capitals, for your information, denote a very proper noun."

"Like I said, I can hardly wait till we get to italics."

"You're incorrigible."

They finished their ice-cream cones, and Adam drove her home. As they went toward the apartment building, Donna saw by the lights in the basement that Jeanie was home, and invited Adam in for coffee.

"I'll take a rain check, if I may. I have a few things to do at Samara. I'll call you tomorrow. Sleep tight."

He gave her a light peck on the cheek, and she left, wondering how she was going to go on seeing Adam without this romance getting out of hand. She had to continue working for him, and she had no intention of not seeing him after hours. Her Gemini ingenuity would be severely taxed.

Chapter Five

On Saturday Donna worked on an outline for a screenplay based on a short story she had written about a single mother.

"I read in that book from the library that television is the major art form of this century," she told Jeanie. "My story should have been a screenplay all along."

"Then how come you've been sitting there for half an hour, frowning at the typewriter?" Jeanie asked.

"It's kind of hard to tell the story, since so much of it takes place inside the heroine's head. I can't have her talking to herself for half an hour. I need another character. Either that, or her six-year-old son has to be precocious enough to discuss adult psychological problems."

"That's probably why the stars always have a sidekick in the successful shows. You know, like Lucy and Ethel. Speaking of sidekicks, you haven't forgotten we're going to play tennis tomorrow?"

"Of course not."

"I thought maybe Adam would want you to go out. I can call someone and we'll have a game of doubles if you like."

"We'll see. Adam said he'd call."

"You could call him."

Donna shook her head.

"You've been out with him," Jeanie persisted. "It's not as though you're begging for a date."

"He said he'd call."

"If he wants you to do something else, go for it. You and I can chase tennis balls anytime."

"I don't break dates with my best friend," Donna said.

"Don't be silly. That's what friends are for. That, and borrowing clothes from."

When Adam finally called, he invited Donna to a barbecue at a friend's house that night. Since he didn't mention Sunday, she waited to see if the subject came up. She and Jeanie were just learning to play tennis, and she wasn't eager to display her lack of skill in front of him, but that wasn't the real reason she didn't mention it. She had never asked a man out and was reluctant to start with Adam.

Jeanie looked at her. "I didn't hear the word tennis," she said.

"I felt shy."

Jeanie just shook her head. "I wonder if 'shy' isn't just another word for proud. You don't want him to know you like him. It's time to hop down from the pedestal, Donna. There aren't any knights in shining armor out there, busting their butts to win us. We're all equal nowadays."

"Some are more equal than others," Donna retorted vaguely.

Jeanie was painting her toenails on the sofa when Adam rang the bell that evening. She had a paper tissue threaded between her toes to prevent smudging. Nail polish, remover, a box of tissues and assorted beauty aids were spread over the coffee table in front of her. With nothing more exciting to do, she was using the evening to perform her beauty chores. She was wearing her housecoat, and her hair was done up turban-style in a towel. "Go up and meet him at the door," she said. "I don't want him to see me like this."

"The poor man is going to begin wondering if I even have an apartment here or just hang out in the lobby," Donna said. But as she was ready and waiting, she went up to meet him.

Adam wore chinos and a blue golf shirt that emphasized his tapering physique and board-flat stomach. His sun-bronzed complexion was the picture of health. Every time she saw him, Donna was surprised that this handsome man was interested in her, but when his eyes glowed in pleasure, she knew he was. As they went out to the wagon, two women getting off the elevator turned around and stared. Donna figured he turned a lot of women's heads.

"You certainly don't keep a guy waiting," he said.

"It can be arranged, if that's what you like."

"That wasn't a complaint!"

Donna noticed that Adam had had the wagon washed. He set out for Highway 37, then turned west. His farm was in the other direction. As they drove into the country, Donna mentioned how pretty and peaceful it was.

She was surprised to see his lips firm in annoyance. "It won't be for long if your uncle gets his way. He's bought up fifty acres out this way the past year, although the zoning is for farmland."

"Then he can't build on them, so what are you worried about? He's probably going to start a hobby farm."

"He's pulled a similar stunt before. He bought four houses in a residential zone and got the city council to change the zoning for him to put up a high rise. It helps when you own a newspaper. He can push his own slanted views on the public. Councillors are politicians. They like to see their names in print, preferably in a flattering light.''

"But Bayville is growing, Adam. He wouldn't be building if housing wasn't needed. People have to have some place to live,'' she pointed out.

"They don't have to pave over prime farmland to do it. It's hard enough to make a living on a small farm. With developers driving the price of land so high, the farmers can't compete. In the end, they're squeezed out completely. If we end up having to import our food, it won't be the cheap prices the consumer pays today.''

"I guess that's for the politicians to worry about,'' she said vaguely.

"And the farmers,'' he added. "I've got a bunch of them organized. When that zone change comes up at council, we'll be there, protesting. But I won't start that discussion, or it'll ruin our evening. As you may have gathered, I tend to become emotional about farming. Samara means a lot to me.''

"How did your parents come to call their place Samara?'' she asked, glad to change the subject. "It sounds sort of exotic. Is it French? I thought maybe it was your mother's name or something.''

"It's from the Latin for key. Not the kind that opens doors, but the seed from certain trees, like maples. We have a lot of them at Samara.''

"That's why you have the keys on the gate. I wondered about that.''

"Actually Mother did name the farm. They have the word *samare* in French. She wanted to call the farm that. Dad wanted to call it The Maples. They compromised.''

"It sounds like your dad did most of the compromising.''

"He would, gladly. He loved her, you see. And she left her home to come here with him. Family means a lot to the

French. Letting her name the farm was a very small price for Dad to pay.''

"It must have been exciting for them," she said, her mind veering off to that long-past time. "Starting a whole new life. Almost like the pioneers."

"I expect there's a good story in it. Why don't you come out to the farm tomorrow and have a talk with Mom? She'll tell you all about it."

Donna was a little in awe of Mrs. Challow, but she felt a genuine stab of regret to have to pass on his suggestion. "I'd love to, but I promised Jeanie I'd play tennis with her tomorrow. You're welcome to join us," she said. In the context, it didn't seem forward. "Do you play?"

"I used to a few years ago. Are you and Jeanie good? I wouldn't want to fall flat on my face."

"If you fall on your face, you'll find both of us right down there on the court with you," she replied, relieved that he wasn't a keen player. "We're just beginners."

"Then it's a date. This is Tom's place," he said, and turned in at a small farm.

The place was neither as large nor as prosperous as Samara. The couple who came out to greet them were about Adam's age. Tom Bennet was a wiry redhead, his wife Marj was a striking blonde two inches taller than her husband, even in her flat-heeled shoes.

"Welcome to Chestnut Bay," she said, shaking Donna's hand. "True, we're not really on the bay, and the chestnut trees are all dying with this new disease, but I like the name."

"What's in a name?" Donna smiled. "I live in the section of Bayville called Riverdale. There's no river in sight, and it isn't in a dale."

"But it sounds good, right? Tom's got the fire going. Come on around and meet the neighbors. I'll see if I can find you a cold beer."

"Oh, I don't drink beer, thanks. Wine will be fine." She noticed that Marj looked embarrassed. She glanced at Adam and saw that he looked embarrassed, too. "Or a cola. Anything."

Marj said, "The budget doesn't run to fine wines, but I can give you a soft drink, if the kids haven't drunk them all up."

About a dozen people were seated on a cedar deck, talking and drinking beer. Children ran around the yard, yelling and playing. The barbecue pit was off to the side of the deck. Marj led them to the deck and served drinks. Adam introduced Donna to his friends. She noticed their faces pinched in displeasure at the name Calvert. "Donna's working for me part-time," he said.

"Would you be related to Mike Calvert at all?" Tom asked.

"A poor relation," she admitted, withholding the word uncle.

Adam rushed in with an amusing story about Rambo, who had caught Joe off guard when he turned his back on him.

"That's the calf you're going to breed, Adam?" Marj asked.

"That's the one. If he's like his father, he'll provide a good strong frame to carry the milk."

Donna was more or less lost as the group, all dairy farmers, talked a little shop. When Marj went to the barbecue, Donna joined her to see if she could help with the cooking. She caught an undertone of financial worries in their talk and expected to see some hamburgers, but it was whole chickens on spits that Marj was cooking.

"I raise these myself," she said proudly. "Free-range birds. You'll find they taste better than the ones you get at the supermarket. Speaking of the supermarket, haven't I seen you clerking there?"

"Yes, I only work at Samara in the mornings."

"How come a Calvert's doing such jobs, if you don't mind my asking?"

"Like I said, I'm a poor relation."

"You might not be as out of place here as I thought," Marj said, and smiled. "Would you mind bringing out the salad, Donna? Annie brought a bowl big enough to feed the whole town. There wasn't room for it in the fridge. You'll find it on the windowsill. I hope it's not all wilted. Since you're just plain folks, I'll treat you like one of us."

"That's the way I like to be treated," Donna said, and went to the kitchen. The table was covered with an assortment of covered bowls and plates, indicating that the wives had pitched in to provide the party. It would have been too much for one to handle. She knew that these women wouldn't have help with the housework, as Mrs. Challow had.

"Sorry about the wine," Marj said when Donna returned with the salad. "We don't go in much for wine."

"That's all right. I'm not crazy about it myself. I just don't like hard liquor, and I never got used to the bitter taste of beer. Do you want me to bring out the other things?"

"Bring anything you can lay your hands on, except the dessert. We'll fetch that later or the kids won't eat their first course."

"Neither will I," Donna said, laughing. "That blueberry pie smells delicious."

"Just between you and me, it's store-bought. Sally works in the office at the school. She doesn't have much free time for baking, but I'm sure they can use the extra money."

Another woman began setting the table, and as they all worked together, Donna felt their former hostility fading. By the time everyone was seated at the long trestle table, she felt right at home. It was a rowdy, good-natured meal. With a dozen children present, the inevitable spills and scoldings occurred, but no one seemed to really mind.

Donna sensed that if she hadn't been there, the conversation might have veered in Mike Calvert's direction, but whenever the subject came up, Adam adroitly diverted it. After dinner the women carried the leftovers into the kitchen. They had used paper plates to lighten the cleaning up, and before long, they rejoined the men for a leisurely second cup of coffee and more conversation. As the sun sank lower in the sky, the younger children became cranky, and soon it was time to go home.

"Don't be a stranger, Donna," Marj said as Donna was leaving. "Drop in any time you're in the neighborhood."

"Thanks, it was a lovely party." She and Adam went to the station wagon and waved goodbye to the other parting guests.

"That really was a lovely party," Donna said as they drove back to town. Night had fallen, and here in the country it was pitch black. The lights of Bayville spread below them in the distance.

"I'm glad you like my friends," Adam said. "It's hard for the ones with a young family to get away, so we have to make our own fun. We usually get together once a month for a big party. Next month, it'll be my turn."

"They'll enjoy the swimming pool," she said. The night was sultry.

"We can have a dip now, if you like." He turned to see if she was interested.

"I'd love it, but I don't have a bathing suit with me."

"It's early. We'll go to your place and get it."

"That sounds good. We don't have a pool at the apartment."

"In that fancy place?" he asked, surprised.

"It's not so fancy."

"Chandeliers, marble—I'd call it pretty fancy."

"The glitz is all on the outside, where it shows."

"Somehow that doesn't surprise me," he said sardonically.

"I get the idea Uncle Mike's not too popular with your friends."

"Farming and residential neighbors are like oil and water. They don't mix. The city people all want to live in the country, but once the place is paved and built up, it isn't country any longer, so they move out farther, till they've gobbled up all the farmland. Before the newcomers are there a week, they're complaining about the smell and the farm vehicles holding up traffic on the road. The farmers complain about dogs and kids pestering their cattle. It's just an all-round bad idea. If you have any influence with your uncle, I wish you'd talk some sense into him."

"I have about as much influence as a mosquito," she said. "I hardly ever see him." She was glad that Adam didn't pursue the subject.

He stayed in the wagon while she ran in for her bathing suit, and they drove immediately to Samara. The lights around the pool were lit, turning it into a shimmering jewel. Cascading pots of flowers and vines were placed at random, adding a grace note.

Mrs. Challow was sitting at an umbrella-covered table by the pool, having a drink, obviously enjoying the evening air. She wore a colorful long and loose gown, and her dark hair was pulled back in a chignon. Donna was always impressed with her style.

"You're back early," she said, welcoming them. "How was the party?"

"Fine," Adam replied. "You should have come, Mom. Everyone was asking for you."

"I hope you told them I had a headache. It's not a lie, just a little inaccuracy of time. I would have one if I had to listen to all those children yelling. I'm too old to do things I don't enjoy."

"We're going to have a swim," Adam said. "You can change in the cabana, Donna. There's a light switch on the left."

"Or you can skinny-dip," Mrs. Challow said archly. "Just pretend I'm not here. Don't scowl, Adam. Your father and I used to do it when you weren't around. My son is a terrible prude," she confided to Donna. "It's the English strain. His ancestors on his father's side were Puritans."

Donna had been afraid that Mrs. Challow would be shocked by her bathing suit, which was cut low at the front and high in the leg, but after her suggestion of dispensing with a bathing suit entirely, she didn't worry. The white suit provided a good contrast to her deepening tan. She noticed with pleasure that her muscles were strong and lean.

She had the idea, when she came out of the cabana, that Adam was appreciating them, too. His gaze lingered on her as she advanced a little self-consciously. He had changed into blue bathing trunks with vivid slashes of red and yellow—their garishness surprised her. It was the first time she had seen him without his shirt and trousers, and she was impressed. The ridged muscles of his stomach looked hard and taut. His chest was lightly patched with dark hair, and his long legs were tanned.

"Don't you have a lovely figure!" Mrs. Challow exclaimed, regarding Donna. "Like a sylph. I used to be slender once, but I'm too lazy to exercise. I still have a small waist, though."

"The water sure looks tempting," Donna said, dipping in her toe.

"Ladies before gentlemen," Adam said, bowing her toward the water.

As quick as lightning, his mother jumped up and pushed him in. A loud cry was followed by a splash as he hit the water. Mrs. Challow laughed loudly as he rose, spluttering. "I love doing that," she said to Donna. "Once I pushed him in when he was wearing his best suit. He was furious."

Donna just stared at these youthful high spirits in a lady of apparent maturity. "I'd better dive in before you push me," she said, and dived in.

They swam back and forth, enjoying the refreshing water after the heat of a summer day. Adam went to the diving board and did a few dives to show off his form. When they were tired, they got out and Mrs. Challow handed them big fluffy white towels. "Would you like something to drink?" she asked. "I've opened a bottle of wine."

"You get your wine after all," Adam said with a smile.

"You like wine?" Mrs. Challow said approvingly to Donna. "I have a French sauternes you must try."

"I'm no connoisseur," Donna told her.

"You'll like this one. I'm surprised the Bennets still aren't serving wine," Mrs. Challow said, shaking her head at such barbarity. "A house wine at least. It costs no more than that wretched beer." She made the word sound profane.

This wine was several classes better than a house wine. Its dry edge left a fruity bouquet in the mouth. Adam urged his mother to tell Donna about her early days on the farm, and she obliged with amusing stories.

"I thought I had never seen any place so bleak," she said, shaking her head. "We arrived in November, when the leaves were gone and the snow had not yet come. *'Quel désastre!'* I cried. I was from Paris, you know, from solid bourgeois stock. We didn't have a neighbor for four miles on either side here, and they did not speak French. The city was hardly even a village, and the cows! What a stench! Ah, how this talk takes me back. We worked like a pair of demons building up the herd, Charles and I. The neighbors came from miles around to help us raise our first barn. The men put it up in one day, and I served them a coq au vin. I don't think they appreciated it. I slaved for hours, slicing mushrooms and peeling little onions and mincing salt pork. I cried when it was mostly all left on their plates.'' She daubed at a tear, but soon resumed her story.

She spoke of freezing in the winter and sweltering in the summer, of broken ploughs and stony fields, of miles of fence to be constructed by hand, and especially about the sense of isolation. It seemed she hated everything about her new life.

''I wonder how you stayed on, Mrs. Challow,'' Donna said.

''Call me Renée. It is not my name, but I detest Honoré. It is much too virtuous for me. I stayed on because of Charles,'' she said simply. ''It was what he wanted, so it was what I had to want, too. And of course I could not admit that I had made a mistake to leave home. I was too proud and foolish. Charles promised that when we were rich, he would build me a bathing pool. That was a great luxury in those days, Donna. At home, only the very wealthy had them. Unfortunately I never learned to swim, but I enjoy my pool. We christened it with champagne. One day I shall learn to swim.''

''You'd better get cracking on it,'' Adam said. ''You've been saying that for as long as I can remember.''

''I am saving it for my old age. One must have something to look forward to. And now I shall go to bed. Victor is waiting for me there,'' she said with an impish grin, and left.

''Victor Hugo,'' Adam explained, when Donna stared in disbelief. ''She's reading *Les Misérables*.''

Donna smiled fondly. ''She's quite a character. She certainly hasn't lost her French élan.''

"She likes to shock people. She also thinks she's annoying me, but she's wrong to call me a Puritan. That story about skinny-dipping, for instance. She doesn't even swim."

"Maybe they just fooled around in the shallow end," Donna said. Adam's smile stretched to a grin. "I mean— you know, fooled around splashing each other," she amended.

"Maybe they did. I know they were happy together, and that's what's important in the long run."

Adam poured another glass of wine, and they huddled into their towels, talking and laughing. It was half an hour later when the lights suddenly went out.

"Mom," Adam said.

"I guess we were making too much noise. Maybe it's a hint we should knock it off."

"You don't know Mom. That's a hint for me to make my move. She's a romantic."

Donna found this a little hard to believe. "It's time for me to be leaving," she said and stood up.

"I'll change in the house," Adam said, and rose, too.

In a few minutes they met again at the pool and went to the wagon. Donna leaned her head back against the seat and closed her eyes, remembering her unusual evening, as the car sped over the pavement. From the rusticity of a country barbecue to the sophisticated French conversation with Mrs. Challow—it was all a little heady.

"I don't know which was more fun, the barbecue or the swim and talking to your mother. She's not what I thought she'd be like at all. She'd always seemed stiff and superior before. I was half afraid of her."

"She just likes to dress up in pretty clothes. She isn't stiff at all. She likes you," Adam said.

"I like her, too. She's a nut, but I like her."

"The act she puts on is sort of a—test, to see if a newcomer is her kind of people."

"Gee, if I was being tested, you should have warned me."

"I don't mean test, exactly. More like feeling you out. If people can't take a little joke, she gets bored with them. Anyway, you passed with flying colors."

"Then it *was* a test, if I passed."

"I think you were testing her, too, subconsciously. You passed a verdict—you said you liked her."

"Maybe you're right."

The wagon drew up in front of her apartment and stopped. Adam pulled her into his arms.

Donna's hair was wet, and the lingering smell of chlorine from the pool wasn't very romantic, either, but when he kissed her, mere reality receded into oblivion. Reality was his lips pressing hungrily on hers, and the glowing flame inside her. It was the feel of firm masculine flesh beneath her fingers, and the encircling warmth of his arms. It was the sense of tender intimacy growing to curling excitement at the building pressure of passion. A kiss had never had such a profoundly disturbing effect on her before. She suddenly knew the truth of that tired cliché, the earth moved.

She slowly withdrew and just looked at him from her dazed eyes. "It must be the wine," she said, bewildered. But two glasses of wine had never made her head swim before.

One finger rose and traced her throbbing lips. "That's one explanation," he said, gazing into her eyes. His voice was husky with desire.

She didn't ask what the other explanation was. She had a feeling she knew. She was falling in love. Or maybe just in fascination. He was a fascinating man. This needed some careful consideration. "See you tomorrow," she said, detaching herself.

He let her go. "What time?"

"One-thirty?"

"Fine." He got out and opened her door. They walked toward the building hand in hand, not talking. Just before he left, Adam said, "You did bewitching things to that white bathing suit."

"I'm glad my money wasn't wasted."

"They should pay you for wearing it."

"You looked pretty good yourself."

"Mom bought that suit. I thought it was kind of goofy, but if you like it..."

"I like it," she said.

She thought he'd kiss her good-night. He lifted her hand and kissed the palm. "See you tomorrow," he said, and left.

She went inside, smiling. What a romantic thing, kissing her hand. No one had ever done that before. This Adam Challow, macho cowboy turned romantic, was quite a revelation.

Adam was smiling as he drove away, too. His mom liked Donna; his friends liked her; and most important, he liked her. This had definite possibilities, but he wanted to know her better before committing himself. The difficult part would be keeping his head. She was so attractive physically that he tended to lose it when he was with her. It was too early to know whether this was love or just physical attraction. Whatever it was, he couldn't remember ever feeling this excited about a woman before.

Chapter Six

"So I'm finally going to get to meet the great Adam Challow," Jeanie said at breakfast the next morning.

"I didn't say he's great, just nice," Donna replied.

"And romantic, sexy, smart, considerate. I'd call that great."

Donna buttered an English muffin and smiled complacently. "Well, maybe he is sort of great," she allowed.

"But I'm still worried about your signs," Jeanie continued. "I mean earth and water. If he's made up his mind, Capricorns are practically immovable. I should warn you, you Geminis are apt to misplace your trust. *You're* impressionable."

"Have I been impressionable in the past?"

"There was that Lit. professor you thought wanted to help you with your writing," she reminded Donna, "but it wasn't writing he had in mind."

"Everybody makes mistakes! How about you and the dentist who forgot to tell you he was married?" Donna retaliated.

"I admit I had a trusting disposition. I'm a Taurus, after all. I'm not saying you and Adam don't suit. The stars don't compel, they just indicate. Anyhow, my horoscope says I'm going to win something today. Maybe I'll beat you at tennis."

"Who are you going to invite to play with us?" Donna asked.

"Mac Davis. Since he sells sports gear, maybe he's interested in sports. I mentioned playing tennis today. I'll give him a call now."

Mac agreed. Donna and Jeanie spent the morning housecleaning. About the only luxury in their apartment was the air conditioning, so they didn't realize just how hot the day was.

"Let's go out for lunch," Jeanie suggested. "It seems a shame to dirty up the apartment when we've just cleaned it."

"Yeah, we might want to invite the guys back after tennis."

"Are you kidding?" Jeanie asked. "I wouldn't invite Mac down here. He's kind of a snob. He's really impressed that Mike is my uncle. I don't want him to see I live in this tacky basement apartment."

"That's silly," Donna jeered. "Why are you going out with him if he's such a snob?"

"Well, he drives a Jag," Jeanie said, then laughed at her own snobbery. "I'd never be serious about him, but he's cute, and he'll introduce me to his friends. Finding a husband is hard work, Donna. You have to employ strategy."

"You make it sound more like a war."

"It is. They call it the war of the sexes. When it goes right, both sides win."

They had lunch at a salad bar, then went home to change into shorts and sneakers. They were just beginners, and didn't belong to any club, so they didn't have proper tennis whites.

When the buzzer sounded, Jeanie said, "I'll meet Mac in the lobby. You might as well come, too. Adam should be here any minute."

"Meeting him in the lobby again," Donna said. "Adam's going to get the idea I'm ashamed of the place, too."

"We'll move upstairs when I get my raise."

"And when I sell my script to television."

They went laughing upstairs. Mac didn't seem such a snob as Jeanie had indicated, although he did wear immaculate tennis whites and designer labels on anything that would hold a label, including the sweatband around his forehead. He was a tall blonde with green eyes.

"I've heard a lot about you, Donna," he said, giving her a firm handshake. "Good luck on the writing."

Adam arrived within minutes. He wasn't dressed nearly as elegantly as Mac, but Donna preferred his more casual if slightly mismatched attire.

"You own Samara, I think?" Mac asked.

"That's right," Adam said, nodding his head.

"I board my horse at your place, Adam. That's a nice setup you have there. The land alone must be worth a lot."

"It is to me," Adam said.

"I own the sports store in town," Mac said. "I'd like to get into riding equipment, but I'm a little short of space. Any chance of buying an acre or so from you to open a shop near the stable?"

"No chance of buying, but I might rent it."

"We'll do lunch some day and talk. I have a partner. I'd have to get it okayed with him. By the way, I've booked us a court at the Hillview for our game, if that's all right with you folks," Mac said, glancing at the others for approval.

Donna and Jeanie usually played at the Y. The Hillview Tennis Club was a very exclusive private club, for members only.

"Great!" Jeanie said. She and Donna exchanged a secret smile. Jeanie would start meeting Mac's friends today.

Adam noticed that smile and wondered at it.

Mac said, "I'll explain to the club that you're my guests. There shouldn't be any trouble about your outfits." He looked uncertainly at their garb. "There is a dress code for members."

"Maybe we should just go to the Y," Donna suggested, and was quickly talked down by Jeanie and Mac.

"Does the Y have an air-conditioned lounge?" Mac asked. That seemed to settle it, and they went to their cars.

"I'm not sure where the Hillview is," Adam said to Mac.

"It's at the south edge of town. Just follow my Jag, Adam."

The couples separated for the short drive. "The Hillview's a very exclusive club," Donna mentioned.

"Mac seems, er, fashionable," Adam said. He wondered if Donna's other friends were all like Mac. Mac seemed the sort of person he had originally taken Donna for, until he got to know her better.

Donna burst into giggles. "Just follow that Jag, or a couple of rubes like us will get lost in Yuppieland."

He relaxed. "I thought we'd seen the last of the Yuppie phenomenon."

"Old Yuppies never die. They just buy away. He must be doing well. Those cars cost a fortune."

"I'll try and be nice to him. Mrs. McAllister mentioned she'd like a riding shop on the premises. There's a log cabin there that could be turned into a shop without much work. It's the house that was on the property when Dad bought it. The house I was born in, actually."

"Like Abe Lincoln," she said.

"They built the present house about five years later."

"I'd like to see the original house sometime."

"You might want to mention it if you decide to write that story about my mother's experiences," Adam suggested.

"I really don't know enough about all that to write it up."

"You know where you can do the research," he said, smiling encouragingly. "I'm sure my mother would be delighted to help you. There's nothing she'd like better than to see her name in print."

"I'll think about it. I'm involved in something else right now. A screenplay for television, actually."

The Jag turned into a driveway, and Adam followed it up an incline to an impressive white frame building that looked like an antebellum mansion. It's sprawling expanse of white siding made a dramatic picture against the surrounding greenery. It had pillars, a fanlit doorway and a wraparound veranda. Groups of tennis players sat on lounge chairs, rackets dangling from their hands as they waited for a court.

They followed Mac's car to the parking lot and got out. "I'll just see if our court's ready," Mac said, leading them on.

There seemed to be almost as many workers at the Hillview as players. Young men and women darted to and fro, each wearing a white shirt with the club's crest on the pocket. An older man carrying a clipboard came up to them.

"Mr. Davis," he said, smiling at Mac. "Your court should be free in half an hour."

"Half an hour!" Mac exclaimed. "I reserved it for two o'clock."

"The Stinsons began their game late," the man said apologetically.

"Oh, well, I suppose if it's the Stinsons," Mac said and turned to explain to his friends. "Doug Stinson is the club president," he said. "Let's watch his game. He's fantastic."

They went to a long bench outside the screened-in court and watched a gray-haired man chase the ball around.

"Great shot, Doug!" Mac called every time the man made a point, and even when he didn't.

The bench didn't have any shade. It was hot and boring watching the game. Half an hour seemed a very long wait. "Why don't we go around to the front and wait on the veranda where there's some shade?" Jeanie suggested. "Or maybe use that air-conditioned lounge?"

"We'll be called any minute," Mac said. He entertained them by examining their rackets and telling them what was wrong with them.

"A little warped, Adam," he said, whipping Adam's racket through the air. "I can put you on to a new lightweight racket. Like a feather in your hand. It's expensive, but worth it. If you're going to play, you need the best equipment, right? Here, try mine. It's imported from Germany."

Eventually Doug Stinson and his partner left the court. "Fantastic game, Doug," Mac called.

"I lost," Stinson growled and brushed past them.

"Great guy," Mac said to Jeanie.

Mac and Jeanie played partners against the other couple and won. Mac was the only real player in the group, but if he was disappointed in his companions' lack of skill, he didn't show it. They played two games, then gave up due to the heat.

"Now for a tall, cool one," he said. "Fantastic game, Adam. Your backswing needs work."

"I felt it was my serve that was weak."

"That, too. And you were a little slow in coming forward for Jeanie's serves. After the first couple, you should have seen she didn't have a clue—that is, her serve was a little weak. The new racket would do wonders for your game."

"I'll think about it," Adam said, holding back a grin. He didn't see how a new racket would suddenly turn him into a pro, but Mac was trying to be friendly, and he went along with his foolishness.

They were grateful to get in out of the sun. The lounge was cool and quiet. It was decorated in a jungle motif, with huge palms set in pots around the room. A mural of lions and tigers enlivened the walls, and the seating was bamboo chairs with imitation zebra cushions.

"This is the Safari Lounge," Mac said with a proud, proprietorial smile as he led them to a central table. "The only place in town you can get a single malt Scotch."

"What's that?" Jeanie asked.

"That's what everyone's drinking now."

"I guess I'm not everyone, then. I'll have a beer," Adam said. "Wine for you, Donna, or a soft drink?"

"They have Perrier if you don't like alcohol," Mac told her.

Donna got the idea Mac didn't want to be at the same table with a plain soft drink. Mineral water did sound good, however, and she and Jeanie ordered that.

While waiting for their drinks, Mac hailed various people who entered the lounge. "Folks, this is Allan Godfrey, the best orthodontist in Bayville," he announced proudly. "Allan, my man. I'd like you to meet my friends. This is Adam Challow. He owns Samara, you know, that big farm outside of town, where we all keep our horses. And these young ladies are Mike Calvert's nieces, Jeanie and Donna Calvert."

Donna noticed that his introductions were all the same. What he stressed was that Adam owned Samara, and that they were Mike's nieces. They had to be somebody important, in other words, just as he had to drive the fashionable car and drink the fashionable drink. Really he was rather pathetic, but he was trying so hard that it was impossible to dislike him.

They had two drinks, then left. "I'm ready for a shower," Mac said. "Of course, we have showers at the club, but since you folks don't have a locker and a change of clothes... I'd be happy to put your name up for a membership if you're interested, Adam. You have to be nominated."

"That's very kind of you, Mac, but I don't have much free time."

"If you change your mind, just let me know. I'll give you a jingle about that store I mentioned. You can fax me your terms if you like."

"No, I can't," Adam laughed. "I don't have a fax machine."

"You should get one. Awesome."

"I make do with the telephone," Adam said, wondering what on earth he would do with a fax machine.

It was with a sense of relief that Donna and Adam escaped from the Hillview into the less-rarefied atmosphere of reality. Adam didn't like to make fun of Donna's friend, so he spoke of other things.

"I notice there's a lot of land available around here," he said. "And it's not good farmland, either. This is where your uncle should build his apartments."

"There must be some reason why he doesn't. Maybe it's too expensive. Or maybe it's zoned industrial."

"The zoning wouldn't bother him," Adam said. But he didn't want to mount his pet peeve. "I have to do my book-keeping tonight. Would you like to grab a quick bite first? Mom has probably prepared dinner already."

"Coq au vin, maybe," she said, remembering last night's conversation. "Lucky you."

"There's always plenty for a guest, if you'd like to join us."

"I'm sorry. But I really do have to work on my screenplay." In fact, she would have liked to have gone, and Adam looked a little disappointed at her refusal. Maybe Jeanie was right. She was too slow. "I'll go home and work. As soon as I shower, that is. The Hillview was impressive, wasn't it?" she said. "I love those big buildings with white pillars. Like Tara or something."

Adam preferred architecture that suited its geography. Tara was out of place in upstate New York. "Is your cousin seriously involved with Mac?" he asked.

"They're practically strangers. She just met him last week."

Were he and Donna practically strangers, too? Maybe she was right. How well did you know a person after one week? He wouldn't have thought Donna would be impressed by a clip joint like the Hillview, for instance, but apparently she was. She had looked thrilled when Mac mentioned it. Maybe she was impressed by Mac Davis, too. Everyone had two sides to his personality.

In Adam's case, he thought of them as his English and French sides, inherited from his father and mother respectively. In simple terms, his English side was the hardworking farmer. His French side was the latent romantic who did foolish things like fly to Paris for a weekend, or buy that motorcycle he seldom used, or fall in love with a woman he scarcely knew. He would subject this budding romance to some hard English scrutiny.

As it was daylight when they parted at the door, Adam didn't kiss Donna goodbye. He just tipped his imaginary hat and said, "See you tomorrow."

"Tomorrow's the day Rambo is leaving. What time are they picking him up, Adam? I want to say goodbye to him."

"Not till ten. I'll miss the young devil."

"But you'll see him at the breeding farm, won't you?"

"Occasionally, but it won't be the same."

"It's funny how you get attached to animals," she said. Now that he was leaving, she wanted to prolong the parting. "Even if they're little beasts like Rambo. Maybe it's their devilishness we like."

She told him about a dog she'd had when she was young. It seemed she hadn't trained it properly, and it chewed up slippers, books, gloves or anything within reach. "But I missed Bingo so much when I went away to school. And now he's gone," she said ruefully.

"You can always get another dog."

"I will, if I ever live in a house instead of an apartment."

Adam soon left. It seemed a good sign that Donna liked animals. There was so much about her he admired that he soon put her seeming admiration for Hillview and Mac Davis out of his mind. It wasn't Donna who was seeing Mac, after all. It was her cousin.

Adam had an opportunity to test the depth of her animal-loving instincts the very next morning. She went to Rambo's stall to say goodbye to him when the vet came to take him away. Rambo was a mischievous fellow, mostly black but with white shoulders and a white blaze on his forehead that gave the effect of a frown.

Adam and Dr. Ivey entered the barn just as she finished feeding the calves. "You can bring Rambo out now, Donna," Adam called.

She opened the bar, and the frisky calf escaped with glee. They had put a rope around his neck, but he moved so quickly Donna didn't have time to grab the rope. He was off, puffing and snorting like a bull ready for the ring. Donna was familiar with his tricks by this time and went after him without fear. She grabbed the rope and led him toward the barn door.

"Frisky little fellow, isn't he?" Dr. Ivey said, running his eyes over the animal. Donna handed him Rambo's rope.

"Good hindquarters. And the eye of a champion," he added, patting the calf's head. Then he glanced down at the legs and bent over. "How are the leg bones?"

Rambo backed away. He didn't like strangers touching him. The rope jerked out of the vet's hand, and Donna reached for it. As she bent over, Rambo lowered his head and bunted her from behind with all the force of his strong body. She went flying, face-first in the dust. Her pink cap flew off. The vet laughed, but Adam darted forward to help her up.

"Are you all right?" he asked.

She turned on her side, rubbing her backside and glaring. "As they say, only my pride is hurt. Wait'll I get my hands on that wretch!"

When he saw that she was unharmed, Adam joined in Ivey's amusement. "Funny place you keep your pride," he said, leaning over to help her up.

Donna saw over his shoulder that Rambo was preparing for another charge, lining up behind Adam with his head down. Rambo never could resist a good target. "Look out!" she called, trying to jump up.

Before she made it, Rambo had rushed forward and butted Adam. He landed on top of Donna, facedown, while Dr. Ivey held his sides and laughed louder. She wasn't aware of his mirth. Adam's weight pressed heavily on her. Their cheeks grazed together. The masculine prickle of incipient whiskers was strangely exciting, and his warm gasps in her ear sent a jolt of adrenaline coursing through her. As he scrambled to rise, his body moved intimately against hers. He pushed the palms of his hands against the earth to lift his shoulders. The thrust of his hips caused a spasm of alarm through her whole body.

She heard a sharp intake of breath and was aware of the masculine scent of him. Every fiber of her being responded to this sudden impact. A shudder shook her body from within. Adam lifted his head, and they were suddenly staring at each other with awful absorption. Rambo, Dr. Ivey—the whole world seemed to have evaporated, leaving them in a strange echoing vacuum. Her lips opened involuntarily, and she tried to fill her lungs, which seemed to have collapsed. Adam looked momentarily stunned. The whole incident didn't last a minute, but it had the force of a revelation.

"Are you all right?" Her voice came out in a whisper.

"Oh, God," he said. His voice was a ragged gasp.

He wanted to make love to her right there, that very instant, on the floor of the barn. Fire had raged through him when he felt her beneath him, her dark eyes gazing into his, half frightened, half excited. If Dr. Ivey hadn't come pelting forward, Adam didn't think he could control himself.

"I hope you two aren't hurt?" Ivey asked, offering his hand. He helped Adam up first. "Sorry I laughed. But it just looked so darned funny...."

"That's all right," Adam said, brushing himself off. His hands were trembling, and when he stole a look at Donna, he saw that she was upset, too.

They all turned to the cause of the mischief. Rambo was examining the ground for food and looking the very picture of innocence.

"Do you still want to kiss him goodbye?" Adam asked Donna.

"Kick him goodbye is more like it after that stunt," she scowled.

Ivey led Rambo out. Adam rescued his hat and Donna's from the dust. He put his own on, then set hers on her head, peak askew. A smile tugged at his lips. "I think he deserves a reward. Mind you, his timing is a little off. It would have been better without an audience, wouldn't it?"

There was no possibility of misreading his meaning. His eyes were glowing with remembered passion. "Your face is dirty," he said, then he turned and followed Ivey out to the truck.

The memory of the sudden, unexpected incident colored the rest of her day. It popped into her mind at odd moments, the banked fire of his eyes as he hovered above her. That ragged "Oh God!" She had thought at first that he was hurt. When she realized he wasn't, she knew the true cause of his outburst and felt exultant.

She didn't see Adam again that morning. She kept listening for his return, but he still hadn't come back at noon, when she left.

Adam thought about the accident, too. He was shaken by that sudden bolt of desire. If she had been anyone but an employee, he might have tried to arrange an affair with her, to see if there was more than physical passion between them. An affair with an employee was not an option. It led to too many complications, but he was determined to continue seeing her casually. Consequently they dropped in on Marj and Tom Bennet one evening, and when Donna suggested double-dating with Mac and Jeanie again, he agreed.

On Thursday evening he invited her to Samara for dinner. Donna seemed so much at home at his table that his doubts were rapidly vanishing. His mother amused them with more anecdotes of her early days on the farm, and Donna began to think she might try an article about it for the farmer's magazine, after she finished her screenplay. Her two jobs and her frequent dates with Adam didn't leave much time for her writing, but she plugged away at it when she could.

The visit of Matt Hibbert loomed large in Donna's mind. Two more story submissions had come thumping back in the mail. She was beginning to feel that the only way to get her writing accepted was by knowing someone in the business. At least Matt could give her some firsthand professional advice.

"Will Adam be picking you up for Uncle Mike's big party?" Jeanie asked when Donna returned quite early Thursday evening.

"I didn't invite him."

Jeanie looked astonished. "Why not?"

"He doesn't like Mike. He and Mike have had a few run-ins." She explained about the developing of the farmlands. "Since Adam's heading a group trying to block Mike's new project, it'd be uncomfortable for them both."

"That's funny," Jeanie said, puzzled. "He doesn't seem to mind that Uncle Mike is Mac's partner in the shop Mac wants to open at Samara."

"You mean *Uncle Mike* is Mac's partner? Adam didn't mention that. I doubt if he knows."

"Mac told him he had a partner. Of course, Mike's only a silent partner, putting up most of the capital, and Mac will run the shop."

"That way Adam wouldn't even have to meet Mike. I'm afraid if they were face-to-face, sparks might fly."

"I suppose it could be awkward," Jeanie said uncertainly. "If you're not going to invite Adam, I have another idea. Uncle Mike asked me to go with cousin Matt, since Matt doesn't know any women in town. I had already invited Mac Davis. Why don't I tell Mike you'll go with Matt? You'll have the whole evening to talk shop. And Adam won't be jealous since Matt's related. I mean, it's really just a family party."

"That's a good idea."

"I'll set it up then." The next question was, "What are you going to wear? Better make it something sensational. Matt's used to consorting with show-biz people."

"I'll be sure to brush the hayseeds out of my hair," Donna said with a smile.

Donna was unhappy about not inviting Adam to the party. In fact, she didn't even want to tell him about it.

What was the point? It would just add another difficulty to a romance that had already had quite enough problems. If he didn't invite her out on Saturday night, she wouldn't say anything about it. And if he did, she'd just have to tell him the truth. He knew she was eager to get on with her writing and would understand she couldn't pass up the opportunity of learning from Matt.

She had sensed some withdrawal in Adam since that fateful encounter in the barn. At times she thought she must have imagined the wild flare of desire that had exploded between them. It had seemed to promise an escalation in the physical side of their relationship, but ever since that day, Adam had treated her differently. He seemed to like her, since he had asked her out a few times, but as she considered it, she realized they hadn't actually spent more than a few minutes alone together. And even then his embraces were lukewarm.

It was all very confusing, and she decided to just forget it and concentrate on the writing.

Chapter Seven

The past few mornings Donna had been painting the white slatted fence around Samara. She worked at it from about ten o'clock, when her early morning chores were done, until noon. She enjoyed the fine weather, the work wasn't mentally demanding, and she welcomed the time it allowed her to think about her writing. She assumed she would be continuing the job that morning, and hoped it wouldn't be too hot. The sky had been overcast and the weather was muggy, but as the day progressed, the sun burned the cloud cover away. When the workers were at coffee break, Adam mentioned a different job.

"I'm taking the spare milking machine over to the breeding farm," he said. "How would you like to come along for the ride?"

It sounded almost like a holiday. She saw Joe smiling into his coffee, and knew that he was thinking the same thing. Favoritism could cause problems between the workers, and she replied, "I could get the fence finished this morning. You don't need me for the trip, do you?"

"You can do the driving. It'd be handy if you learned to drive the wagon and could run some of the errands from time to time. You should learn where the breeding farm is. It'll give you a chance to say hello to Rambo."

The memory of that interlude brought a blush to her cheeks. "I'm not sure I want to renew my acquaintance with that critter," she said. "How far away is the farm? I'd have to come back here after and pick up my van."

"You'll be back in plenty of time. It's not that far."

"I'd better wash up then," she said, and rose to go to the outdoor tap.

"Why don't you use the washroom inside?" he suggested. "You might want to use the mirror to brush your hair."

Donna removed her boots and went into the kitchen. She had used the washroom off the kitchen a few times before.

Outside, Joe said, "Pretty hot for her to be working in the sun today. That last stretch of fence has no shade. She might get sunstroke. You want me to finish the fence?"

"It's too hot for you, too, Joe."

"Donna's working out pretty well," Joe mused. "Has a real way with the heifers. Doesn't mind hard work. Seems like you were worried about nothing, eh, Adam? I mean, she's not like the other Calverts."

"Donna doesn't have much to do with them," he said dismissively.

"No, she's a nice girl. Only she doesn't like to be called a girl."

"She's not a girl."

"Nice woman," Joe said obligingly. "I'll go and fill the feeding machines. We need lime for the feed. You might pick it up at the co-op store on your way back."

"I've got it on my list."

"Right. See you this afternoon."

When Donna came out with her face clean and her hair brushed, Adam stood up. "All set?"

Aware of his eyes studying her, she wished she wasn't wearing her paint-smeared clothes. "I feel a little grubby in my work clothes, but this *is* a work trip. Isn't it?" she added.

"That's right. Only you've been upgraded to my chauffeur."

"Then I'd better wear my cap," she said, and put it on.

Adam didn't say anything, but he reached out and removed it. He put his hand on her elbow and then went to the wagon. "It's an automatic, so you shouldn't have any trouble," he said, opening the driver's door.

"I'm the chauffeur. Shouldn't I be opening your door?" she pointed out.

"I don't want you forgetting you're a woman just because I'm letting you drive my wagon." He handed her the keys.

There wasn't much danger of forgetting it when he looked at her like *that.* She slid onto the leather seat, and Adam got in at the other door. "We'll leave the windows closed and turn on the air conditioning since it's so muggy," he said.

Donna reached to insert the key, but before she started the engine, she turned to Adam. "I hope that's not why I'm along for this ride. Because of the heat, I mean. I don't mind working in the heat, Adam. That's what I'm paid for."

She knew by the faint flush around his ears that he had invented an excuse for her to go with him. "It'll be useful for you to know where the farm is," he insisted.

Donna didn't persist, but she determined then and there that she wouldn't make a habit of taking this sort of favor from him.

Adam decided it was best to avoid personal conversation for the time being, and talked business instead. He described the work of the breeding syndicate, explaining that it worked with the local agricultural college, developing new improved strains of feed grain as well as trying to improve the milk yield of cows by selective breeding. When they arrived, Adam went to the office to discuss business with the manager, and one of the students gave Donna a tour of the facilities.

His name was Mark. He was a husky blonde. Donna wasn't surprised that Mark praised Samara. She already had the idea that it was the most modern and profitable dairy farm in the area. What did surprise her was that Rambo remembered her and came forward to have his head rubbed.

"He likes you," Mark said, studying Rambo. "Wonderful conformation, but his temper's pretty volatile. Of course, he's young. Maybe he'll grow out of it."

"Meanwhile, I suggest you not turn your back on him," she warned.

"It must be nice working at Samara," Mark said later. "Especially when the boss gives you such soft jobs." His knowing eyes laughed conspiratorially. Donna felt like a kept woman.

After the tour, Adam soon joined them, and they went to the wagon. Mark got the milking machine out and took it around to the barn.

"I'll drive if you like," Adam said, opening the passenger door.

"At least let me drive, since that's why I'm here," she snipped. She went to the other side to let herself in.

Adam knew that Donna would never use her charms to get favors from him, but her attitude this morning proved that she was positively against anything of the sort. It raised her even higher in his estimation.

As they cruised back to Samara, he said, "What would you like to do tonight? Why don't we take the boat out, since it's so muggy."

"I wouldn't be surprised if it rains," she said. "I should have finished that fence this morning."

"But if it doesn't rain..."

"Yes, all right," she said, almost angrily. If a stranger like Mark realized she was being given special treatment, what must the other workers at Samara think? "But if it does rain, I should stay home and work on my screenplay."

"How is it coming?"

"It still has the charm of novelty for me, but to be realistic, I don't suppose it'll be snapped up by the networks."

"Did you ever think of offering it to the local cable company?"

"No, I guess I want to start at the top," she replied.

"Everyone has to pay their dues."

"Unless they're lucky enough to be born into a good job," she said.

Adam took it as a slur on his own inheritance of Samara and didn't offer any more suggestions. She was in a bad mood by the time they reached Samara, but there was no point trying to explain it to Adam. She had already snapped at him a couple of times. He just repeated that she should know where the breeding farm was, although she'd never had to go there before and probably wouldn't have to again.

It was just twelve—time for her to leave—when they reached Samara. She went directly from the wagon to her van. Adam went with her and held the door.

"See you tonight, if it doesn't rain," she said from the open window. A northern wind was blowing in dark clouds, but the approaching storm might be over by evening.

"Drive carefully," Adam said, then he stood watching as the rust-spotted van chugged down the driveway.

The store was always busy on Friday with the beginning of the weekend rush. That day, tempers were short because of the weather. Every half hour or so someone in the express line would start an argument with someone who had more than eight items, and Donna was called in to referee. The clanging of the cash register and the sickly green of the overhead lights was giving her a headache. She hardly had a minute to think and was tired by the time her shift was over. The store had a special on watermelons so Donna took one home. When she went to the van, it was raining. It wasn't a quick violent shower, but a slow drizzle that hung on till evening.

At seven Adam called. "Nice night for a boat ride," he said facetiously. "What would you like to do instead? There's a French film festival on."

"I'm not into French films. I think I'll stay home and work on my play, Adam." He was about to persist when she added, "I'm tired."

"If that's what you want," he said, disappointment in his voice. "Mom would probably like to see the movie. I'll ask her. How about tomorrow night? I thought we might go to a club, kick up our heels. Dancing," he added enticingly.

It sounded like fun. Donna sensed that Adam was trying to appease her, even though he wasn't aware of having done anything wrong. Maybe it wasn't so wrong of him to try to make her life a little easier. And now she had to confess about going to Uncle Mike's party, and not asking him.

"I'm busy tomorrow night, Adam," she said. The edge of annoyance in her voice was due to her private worries, but Adam had no way of knowing that.

"Have I accidentally offended you, Donna?" he asked. "If I have, I wish you'd just come out and tell me what it is. I feel as if I'm walking on eggshells—and smashing them."

"No, you haven't done anything—except try to pamper me."

"What is it, then?" After a brief pause he said, "Have you got another date?"

"I'd hardly call it a date. It's my uncle's twenty-fifth anniversary party. Sort of a family thing."

"Your Uncle Mike?" he asked.

"Yes. I didn't think you'd like to go."

"It wouldn't be my first choice for a Saturday night out," he admitted. The idea certainly didn't appeal to him one bit, but if he and Donna were going to be seriously involved, he'd have to learn to accept her relatives. "I might go if you asked me very nicely," he said, to lighten the mood.

"I wouldn't subject you to it. Maybe we can do something Sunday. That boat ride we missed tonight . . ."

Adam really wanted to see her. The little knot in their relationship bothered him. "What about Saturday afternoon?" he suggested. "We could take a picnic to Elbow Island. Do you do any fishing?"

"Not if I can avoid it. Drowning worms isn't my idea of fun. Why don't you and Joe go? He mentioned he likes fishing."

"Fishing wasn't really the point of it," Adam said.

She sensed the air of injury in his voice and wanted to finish this conversation before it deteriorated any further. "I'm pretty busy all day Saturday, Adam. There are relatives coming from out of town. And I have to drum up something to wear. You know how it is."

"Are your parents coming?" he asked with interest. It seemed like a good chance to meet them, and he decided he would go to the party after all.

"No, they couldn't make it."

"Oh."

"So you'll call me about Sunday?"

"Sure. Have a good time at the party."

"I will. Bye."

"Goodbye."

She hung up the phone, completely dissatisfied with the way things had turned out. Sunday she'd apologize and explain anything that needed explaining.

"You look as if you've just lost your best friend," Jeanie said. "Was that Adam?"

"Yeah. He would have come to Mike's party if I'd asked him. I think I'll call him back and invite him."

"A major breakthrough!" Jeanie said approvingly. Then she frowned, "What about Matt?"

"Matt's our cousin. It's not a date. He'll come with us."

"But what fun would it be for Adam, you talking shop to Matt all night, and him surrounded by Calverts, whom he cordially dislikes?"

"I guess you're right. It wouldn't be fair to Adam, but I feel sort of—I don't know. I feel badly about it."

"It's that vivid Gemini imagination of yours. You tend to go to extremes emotionally. Adam's probably already asked somebody else out."

"Thanks a lot, Jeanie."

"I know what we'll do to cheer you up. Let's dig into our closets and decide what to wear tomorrow night. Something really special. That'll take your mind off Adam."

Jeanie grabbed her cousin's hand and physically pulled her up from the sofa. When they were rooting through their closets, Donna managed to push Adam to the back of her mind. It'd be all right on Sunday.

"I'm definitely wearing black," Jeanie said. "It's dramatic on blondes. You brunettes look better in bright colors. What about that red dress you wore to the prom our last year in college?"

"Too fancy. White suits me. In the summer, I mean."

"Your white open-backed dress! With my blue-and-silver shawl. Perfect!"

They rushed around, assembling their dresses and accessories and trying them on. Jewelry and hairdos were discussed and tried until they were both satisfied. Donna was going to wear her hair pinned up for the occasion.

"We'll be the most gorgeous pair there," Jeanie said.

"And the most modest," Donna added, laughing. Her cousin always got carried away.

They spent the remainder of the evening doing their nails and some odd beauty chores. At eleven-thirty, they had some watermelon and went to bed.

When they rose in the morning, the sun was shining. The trees and grass outside looked fresh from the recent rain. They had to choose an anniversary present for their aunt and uncle. Jeanie volunteered to do this while Donna worked on her writing. Shopping was Jeanie's second favorite hobby, after men. "To shop is human, to find a bargain, divine," she said as she slung her purse over her shoulder.

It was nearly noon when Jeanie came back with a large crystal punch bowl. "What do you think?" she asked, setting it on the kitchen table, where its baroque splendor looked incongruous in their modest kitchen.

"It's pretty."

"It'll look better in Mike's house. It's hard to buy for people who have everything. I wanted to get something for both of them, and that pretty well limits it to a present for the house. I figured even if they already have one, you can always use another punch bowl." Donna looked surprised. "I mean for occasions like Christmas when you serve punch, there are usually dozens of people around."

"I think it's nice. Let's wrap it now and get it out of the way before it gets broken."

It took nearly half an hour to do a fancy job of wrapping the huge box in silver paper. When it was done, it was time for lunch.

The phone rang while they were clearing the table. Jeanie ran to answer it. Donna thought it might be Adam and waited eagerly to be handed the phone.

It was Matt Hibbert. He had arrived that morning. Mike had to go out that afternoon, so he suggested Matt call his cousins and spend the day renewing his acquaintance with them since they hadn't seen each other for several years.

"Why don't you come over this afternoon, Matt?" Jeanie said. "In fact, I'll pick you up."

"Not necessary. I have my own wheels. Just give me the address, and I'll find you."

She gave him the address, told Donna what was going on, and they both scrambled around tidying the apartment and themselves for his arrival.

"I wonder what he looks like now," Donna said as she put on lipstick at the mirror. "He was kind of thin and scrawny in the old days."

"He used to look like a rooster," Jeanie said. "Remember, that beaky nose, eyes close together and his little pointed chin?"

"With dark red crimped hair," Donna added.

"He can't have gotten his looks from his mother. Dora's the roly-poly type," Jeanie said, admiring herself in the mirror.

The buzzer sounded while they were finishing their preparations, and Donna darted to answer it.

She knew Matt had been in Los Angeles, and so she wasn't surprised that he appeared at their door in blue-tinted sunglasses, a pink shirt and fashionable white trousers. She recognized the face, but what surprised her was that he had straight blond hair.

"Is that you, Matt?" she asked.

"Hey, I've got to be somewhere," he said, and planted a cousinly kiss on her cheek.

He strode into the apartment, lifted his blue glasses for a quick look around and said, "Great set for a horror movie. Shall we split before the atmosphere depresses the hell out of us?"

"Oh, I thought—"

Jeanie came darting into the hallway and stopped dead. "Matt, is that you?" she asked.

"Alive and in person. The toothpaste's out of the tube now. No point in trying to hide it. You must be Donna."

"I'm Jeanie."

Donna said, "I'm Donna."

He pointed at them. "Jeanie, Donna, got it in one take. We'll call it a wrap."

"But you didn't used to be a blonde," Jeanie said. It occurred to Donna that he didn't used to be so affected, either.

"And you ladies didn t used to be gorgeous. Let's not knock progress, babe. I had it bleached and straightened. Shall we split this scene?"

"Donna wanted you to look at a screenplay she's writing," Jeanie said.

"Whoaa! Cool the jets. This guy's on holiday. But hey, seeing it's you, I'll give it the once-over, babe. Do we have to do it here?"

Donna already had the idea that Matt wasn't going to be much help. "Where do you suggest?" she asked.

"Uncle Mike has a cee-ment pond at his place. He suggested we go back there."

"That sounds great. We don't have a pool here," Jeanie said.

"My God, you don't even have a pool?" Matt said, staring as if it were a floor that was missing, or indoor plumbing. "Grab your suits, ladies, and I'll get you both out of here."

They got their swimsuits, Donna picked up her script, and they went out into the sunlight. A group of young boys was huddled around a low-slung red sports car.

"Is that your car?" Jeanie exclaimed.

"Hey, if you've got it, flaunt it."

"What is it?"

"A Ferrari, like the one Tom drove in *Magnum*. Tom Selleck."

"It only holds two," Donna pointed out. "We'd better take our van."

"And leave this for the rabble to destroy?" Matt asked, slanting his blue glasses at her. "No way, babe. Blondie and I will go in the Ferrari, you follow us. Then I won't have to drive anyone home. Sorry I can't take both of you, but you'll get to drive in the Ferrari tonight. I think Mike said you're the one who couldn't get a date? The guys around here must be blind," he added, to appease her.

"I could get a date!"

"Right, of course. So you'll follow us. You know where Mike's place is?"

"Yes, I know where it is."

"Just look, don't touch, kids," Matt said, smiling tolerantly at the boys around his car. He opened the door for Jeanie and the car took off like a rocket.

Donna consoled herself that at least she wouldn't have to hear herself called babe all the way to Mike's house. Matt was probably just trying to impress them with his Hollywood manners. His brain couldn't have rotted entirely in a few years. Once he settled down, he really could help her a lot with her script. He must be smart, or how could he be so successful?

Mike Calvert lived in a sprawling mansion on the northwest side of town. It was a Mediterranean-style house of white stucco with a red tile roof. It looked splendid in summer, although Donna thought it must look cold and out of place in winter. She went around the side of the house to the pool. Matt had driven so quickly that he and Jeanie were already changed and sitting at a big round table by the pool.

She didn't bother to change, but just joined them. "I brought my script," she said rather shyly.

"Yet another struggling writer," he said, with a shake of his head. "Happens every place I go. I think the whole world wants to be a TV writer. But what the heck—family. I'll give it a gander for you."

"Thanks," Donna said.

Matt tossed the script aside and said, "How do we get service around here?"

"This isn't a hotel," Jeanie said. "If you want something to drink, I'll go and get it."

"A martini for me."

"Soda water," Donna said, when Jeanie looked at her.

Donna picked the script up and handed it to Matt. "Since you're not going to be here very long, and there's the party tonight, maybe you wouldn't mind having a peek at this now. I really appreciate it, Matt," she added.

He gave her the same tolerant smile he had given the boys ogling his car, but he did begin looking at the script.

"Too static an opener," he said, after a minute. "You want to open with a bang, an attention-grabber, or the audience will just flip that old dial. I mean, a woman called Anne, washing dishes... Why not just put her in bed asleep? That's what it'll do to your audience."

"I guess it is kind of a dull opening," she said.

"Only way to handle it would be a voice-over, and that's ancient history. People want action."

"It's supposed to set the scene. You know, a woman thinking about her life, having to work hard to raise her kids alone."

"Couldn't she do this thinking in a hot tub, or a bubble bath?" Donna stared at him. "Hey, I'm not suggesting FFN."

"What?"

"Full frontal nudity. Not for TV. A discreet rear shot."

"She doesn't have a hot tub. Besides, it wouldn't establish the mood. I read in a book I'm studying—"

"Forget the books, babe. Listen to Cousin Matt. Maybe if you just gave me a summary of the plot," he said, shoving the script aside.

"It's about a woman whose husband died, leaving her with a young son to raise."

"Zzzzzzz," he said, closing his eyes and feigning sleep. "Done to death, babe. Get with the program. You've got to do better than that. You need a twist, a high concept."

"Oh," she said, utterly confused. "Well, it is kind of a common problem. I think a lot of women would be interested."

"Depends on how Anne—we'll change her name to Stephanie—solves this problem."

"She has to work, of course. She gets a job in a school, then she worries about not being home enough with her little boy. The son gets into trouble, and—"

He lifted his hand. "Stop. I can hear the sets clicking off from here. We need a twist. How about she turns hooker?"

"Oh, no! It's not that kind of story, Matt. She's just an average woman."

"Average doesn't cut it. Who wants to watch average? But you think the hooker thing's been overdone, you just might have a point. How about she turns to blackmail?"

"Who would she blackmail?" Donna asked.

"You'd have to change her job. Now, if she was a psychiatrist, she'd have inside dope on her clients. They could be VIPs. Movie stars, politicians."

"But if she were a psychiatrist, she wouldn't have to resort to blackmail. She'd be well off."

"Right, she has to keep the audience's sympathy. You mentioned the kid in trouble. Say he needed a very expensive operation. Or had some rare disease."

"This was more of an everyday story, Matt."

Jeanie arrived with the drinks, and Matt handed Donna her script back. "Why don't you do a rewrite along the lines we've been discussing, and we'll talk later? You've got to bump up the sperm count. I'm being brutally frank with you, babe, but I know you wouldn't want it any other way. This script just doesn't do it for me. You fix it up, and I'll get some actresses I know to give it a read. Or I can recommend a good script doctor, if you don't feel you can handle it."

He went on to recommend some bimbos whose fame was based solely on their bodies as the lead character. Donna realized that she and Matt were on completely different wavelengths, and wrote him off as a mentor. She soon realized that he would make a good comic character, however, so she just watched and listened, studying him for future use in a different script or story. Actually she was beginning to feel that the screenplay wasn't her medium. It was always internalized writing that she enjoyed, and that she wrote best.

Matt talked about his work with various stars, and was amusing, even if she didn't believe half of what he said.

"You didn't drive all the way from L.A., did you?" Jeanie asked. "I was just wondering how come your car is here."

"I winged in and rented the wheels in New York. I actually drive a Mercedes. Red convertible. But hey, I've gotta let the old crowd know the local boy's made good. I could hardly drive up in a taxi. Image is important. You should remember that, Donna. When you come to L.A., you want to hype up your image. Don't tell anyone you've been clerking in a supermarket."

"I also work on a farm," she said.

"She feeds the calves," Jeanie told him.

Matt found this hilarious. "Maybe you should do a remake of the *Beverley Hillbillies*," he said. "What's your boss like? Jed Clampett?"

"More like Gary Cooper," Jeanie told him.

"Ah, a sparkling conversationalist." Matt laughed.

"Yup," Donna said.

They finished their drinks and had a swim. Matt dropped his Hollywood act at times and became almost likeable. Donna felt that if he were visiting for a week instead of two days, he might come down out of the clouds long enough to help her, but he was leaving Monday. She meant to spend Sunday with Adam, so it seemed nothing would come of this, after all.

At five she and Jeanie went home in the van. Matt, who wanted to be seen around his hometown in the rented Ferrari, said he'd pick Donna up at six-thirty for Mike's barbecue.

Chapter Eight

Around seven in the evening, Adam began wishing he *had* gone with Donna to her family reunion. He'd been spending so much of his free time with her, he was now at loose ends on a Saturday night. He hoped he hadn't offended Donna by refusing to go to her family gathering. She certainly hadn't put any pressure on him. Well...she hadn't really *invited* him. He decided that was because she knew about his feelings for Mike Calvert.

His mother had declined the invitation to the French film festival, saying, "In this heat, I'll just sit by the pool and watch the sun set. When the stars come out, I'll go inside and read. I am bored with Victor. I shall read a modern novel instead. But you know, Adam, if you catch the second show, you might also catch Donna on her way home from the family party afterward. I doubt the party will break up before midnight."

His smile admitted this thought had crossed his mind.

Adam had a swim, then worked in his office until eight-thirty. The film festival drew only a small crowd on a Saturday night in summer. The English subtitles were distracting, but Adam stayed until the end, then called Donna's apartment. There was no answer. He didn't think she would be home and in bed so early, so he decided to have a cool beer at a pub and call again in half an hour.

He met Tom Bennet there, watching baseball on television. Marj had taken the kids home to visit her mother, and he had found the house lonely without them, so he'd gone out. Adam had a drink with Tom, then phoned Donna again at eleven-thirty, still with no answer.

At a quarter to twelve, he figured he'd drop by the apartment building and wait a few minutes instead of phoning. He might get lucky and catch her returning. If not, he'd just go home. He drew up at the curb across the street and parked his car in the shadows of the tall trees at five to twelve. He'd wait till midnight. He hoped she'd come. The day seemed ninety hours long without her. Adam knew that if he did see her tonight, he'd tell her he was serious about her. Maybe not actually propose—he'd hardly known her long enough for that—but he'd give her some idea of his feelings and see if she felt the same way. It was becoming more difficult to hold himself back every time he was with her.

He thought about his time with Donna. He liked everything he had learned about her. She was honest, dependable, hardworking and fun. But even if she were none of those things, he'd still love her. It gave him a warm feeling to know that even though he was also bowled over by physical attraction, he still wasn't making a mistake. Now, if she just felt the same way!

Mike and Dora's anniversary party was about what Donna had expected. Besides the relatives, several friends and business colleagues attended. Mike spent most of his time with the latter, which seemed like a strangely unromantic way to celebrate twenty-five years of marriage. Mike hardly glanced at his wife, although he had given her a diamond bracelet before dinner. Dora had given him a gold watch, as impersonal as a corporation retirement gift.

The crowd was too large for a sit-down meal. Dinner was a barbecue around the pool, but it wasn't anything like the barbecue Tom and Marj Bennet had thrown. Dora had hired a catering company to cook and tend the bar. All the guests had to do was tell how they wanted their steak done, then sit at a table and wait for it to appear before them. Half the fun of a barbecue was the cooking.

There weren't many younger couples there, so Jeanie, Donna and their dates all sat together. Mac Davis seemed impressed by Matt's Hollywood act.

"This is the life," Mac said. "Mike really knows how to throw a party."

"All it lacks is some talent in bikinis," Matt added.

"I guess it seems pretty tame to you, Matt," Mac said, urging him to relate his Hollywood experiences.

"I'll tell you, Mac, we had a wrap party last week for a TV movie I was working on—twenty, count 'em, twenty— bathing beauties. The most beautiful women in America— heck, in the world—flock to Hollywood. I won't tell you who ended up in the pool in his new silk suit."

"You?" Mac asked obligingly.

"In person. With a blonde on either side. What a night! A good thing my Rolex is waterproof," he said, flashing his expensive watch.

Donna and Jeanie exchanged tight little smiles. Donna didn't know which was worse, this business dinner masquerading as an anniversary party, or the wild party Matt was talking about.

At around nine-thirty, a combo began playing, and the couples danced on the patio. The music wasn't very exciting, though, and after a couple of dances, Jeanie took pity on Donna and changed partners.

"It doesn't seem fair, you having to dance with your cousin all night," she said.

Donna didn't consider Mac much of an improvement, but at least it was a change. "Are you making any progress on that shop you want to set up at Samara?" she asked. "I haven't seen you around the farm."

"I still have to straighten out a few points with my partner. Mike's so darned busy. I'll have a word with him tonight, if I get the chance. I'll be giving Adam a buzz next week. Mike's not too happy about renting the shop. He always prefers to buy, but this time he sees a good chance for profit so I think he'll go for it. Your cousin's a great guy, by the way. He's going to give me a game at Hillview tomorrow. Maybe you'd like to come along? Jeanie's coming."

"Thanks, Mac, but I have other plans."

"If they involve Adam Challow, bring him, too. The more the merrier. He and Mac would hit it off great."

Donna hardly knew how to talk with anyone so blind to reality. But it was kind of Mac to offer, and she said, "Thanks, I'll ask him."

By eleven, Donna's head was splitting from the loud music. She'd danced with some of her other relatives, all older men, who were charming but out of shape. Her last dance had been with old Uncle Fred, and when she was through she returned to her table and suggested they should go home. Matt was gaining a lot of attention, and she felt he wasn't too eager to leave, but by a quarter to twelve, he had finally had enough.

Matt and Donna led off, with Mac and Jeanie following. They soon drew up in front of the apartment and stopped. They all got out and stood, talking.

"The night's young," Matt said. "What do you say we go somewhere for a drink?"

"You've had enough to drink, babe," Donna said. They were all calling each other babe by this time, as a joke.

"Aw, shucks," Matt said, "you don't have to git up at dawn and milk the cows tomorra, lass."

"If you want to come in, we'll make some coffee," she suggested.

"Into the apartment from hell," Matt said, grimacing.

Mac Davis, who had never been there, said, "I can't believe a Calvert is living in squalor."

"It's atmosphere for our writer," Matt explained. "Donna's the changeling of the family. Did you know she's a farmhand, Mac?"

"He knows," Donna said. "And don't laugh. It's great experience. I'm learning all kinds of interesting things."

"If you say so, babe," Matt laughed. He enjoyed razzing her. "What are you learning out there in the pea patch?"

"You should see her decked out for work," Jeanie said. "She stumbles out of bed at the crack of dawn and has to wear big army boots. And comes home smelling like—well, need I say more?"

"Don't knock those boots. They were a present from my boss," Donna said, refusing to take offense.

This got a good laugh. "Wouldn't surprise me none if the rascal went whole hog and gave you an apron for your birthday."

Donna refused to be intimidated. "Aw, shucks, I was hoping for new overalls," she said.

"You want to learn the language of the barnyard while you're there," Matt said. "For your writing, I mean. I reckon Pa Kettle doesn't walk on the farm; he moseys on over to the back forty."

"Wasn't it you who suggested I do a rewrite of the *Beverly Hillbillies?*" Donna reminded him.

"Bad casting," Matt said. "I forgot about your boss. Gary Cooper."

"Yup," Donna said, and they all laughed as they went into the apartment together.

Across the street, Adam sat with the window down, listening. His temper rose higher at every word. He was already upset to see Donna arrive in a flashy sports car with a fashionable young man who passed, at least in the dark, for handsome. He soon recognized Mac Davis as the other man. Some family party! She'd probably never even gone to her uncle's. She had certainly talked Adam out of joining her. Now he knew why.

In fact, he knew why a Calvert was at Samara in the first place—just collecting research for her writing. No wonder she had never shown any true interest in writing his mother's story. She just wanted to poke fun at their country ways.

He had thought she was really something special, and all the time she was using him. Holding him up to ridicule as Pa Kettle to her real friends. How had he been such a chump? She had fooled them all. Joe, his mother, the other workers—they all liked her. He should have recognized her for what she was when she first came calling in her diamond bracelet and her fancy riding outfit.

Adam turned the key and the station wagon shot forward with a squeal of tires. He hardly noticed where he was going; he just wanted to put some miles between himself and Donna. When he noticed he was on the highway, he drove for twenty-five miles through the night, trying to cool off his temper. He reviewed all their past relationship, and found many questionable items.

Funny Donna had never asked him into her apartment, for instance. It was hard to play the poor girl when you lived in a fancy building with a marble foyer and a chandelier. But what really hurt him was that she was making fun of him;

laughing at him behind his back with her city friends. He was too proud to forgive that. And he was angry enough to want revenge. No more pampering her at work. Let her earn her keep, like the others.

Donna was really looking forward to her Sunday date with Adam. When the phone rang early Sunday morning, she jumped out of bed to answer it.

"Good morning, Donna. I hope I didn't wake you up," Adam said.

She thought it must be the dregs of sleep that made his voice sound so different. It was loud and hearty, but it wasn't friendly.

"As a matter of fact, I was still in bed. What time is it, anyway?" she asked, rubbing her eyes.

"It's nearly nine, sleepyhead. You must have had a late date at that family reunion."

A glance at her watch told her it was not quite eight-thirty. "No, not particularly," she replied.

"How did it go, anyway?"

"It was pretty bad. I was glad you weren't along."

"I'm sorry you didn't enjoy yourself." He bit back a mention that she certainly seemed to be enjoying herself when she came home, because he didn't want her to know he had been waiting.

"What did you do?"

"I managed to amuse myself. Sorry if I got you out of bed."

"That's all right." She looked out the window and saw the sun shimmering through the branches outside. "It's a nice day, anyway. Do you want to take the boat out?"

"I'd like to, but something's come up. I'm afraid I won't be able to make it today."

"Oh," she said, disappointed. "What do you have to do? Will it take all day?"

"I'm afraid so. A little trip out of town, actually. Have to see a man about a cow."

"Maybe I could go with you," she said, wondering where he could be going.

"I'm sure you'll find something more amusing to do."

"Mac and Jeanie are playing tennis. I suppose I could join them," she said. She wanted to repeat that she'd rather go with Adam, wherever he was going, but she had already said it once. To insist went against her nature.

"That's a good idea. See you tomorrow, usual time?"

"I'll be there at six-thirty."

"See that you're not late," he said, and hung up.

Donna sat frowning at the receiver. Had she heard that right? "See that you're not late." What kind of a parting was that, when he was breaking a date they'd been looking forward to for two days? Adam must have gotten up on the wrong side of the bed this morning. Or maybe there was some trouble at the farm, a valuable cow sick or something. That could be it.

Since she was up and wide awake, she didn't bother going back to bed. Sunday was a long day to get in alone, and with her recent disappointment about her television script, she wanted a while to think about her writing before going on to something else. Maybe there was a little something in what Matt said. A story did become rather dull when you stuck to reality.

She decided to go to Hillview with the others, after all. Maybe she could talk some sense into Matt. He had mentioned PBS did dull scripts like hers. He hadn't actually called it dull, but that's what he meant. She'd see if she could get a name of someone to send her script to at least. It would help pass the day, which seemed to stretch before her as a long, lonesome period.

She made bacon and eggs when she heard Jeanie getting up, and they discussed their evening over breakfast.

"I won't be seeing Adam, after all," she said. "He's busy today."

"On Sunday?"

"I guess something came up at the farm."

"Capricorns are very practical, hard workers. Business before pleasure."

"He sounded kind of miffed."

"Well, he's human, too. He's probably disappointed. Why don't you spend the day with the rest of us then, babe?"

"Aaargh! Only if you promise not to use the B word."

"You got it. Mac's picking me up at one. Why don't you give Cousin Matt a jingle?"

She phoned Mike's house, but Matt was still asleep. Her cousin called back around eleven and said he'd pick her up at one. The day was better than she expected. They played doubles, had a drink in the Safari Lounge, then Jeanie and Mac had a game of singles, and she finally got Matt to talk sensibly about her writing.

"You don't have to impress me with how well you're doing, and all that Hollywood jargon, Matt," she said. "Just give it to me straight. Is there any chance of selling anything that isn't all glitz and glamour? As you must know by now, I don't know anything about that kind of world."

"I guess I went overboard on trying to impress people with how well I'm doing," he admitted. "You want the lowdown? Writing for television is like anything else. It has to be good. And to be good, it has to come from the heart. I didn't feel your story about the working woman was very good. It was trite. Strictly formula. It sounds corny as hell, but why don't you write about what you know, Donna?"

"But I don't know very much—yet, I mean. There's so much I haven't done."

"The only time I see your eyes light up is when you talk about that farm, and especially that farmer. I think you know something about love."

"Boy meets girl? How trite can you get?"

"It's been done a million or so times," he admitted.

"And it'll be done another million. That's why you have to make your story special."

"It's really the story that appeals to me more than the scriptwriting."

"Then write your story, and if it's really good, the script-writers will do the screen treatment. What opened the door for me was a little story about myself, who else? The incident happened on my tenth birthday, and it involved a bicycle I'd wanted for a year. Dad had lost his job the week before my birthday. It looked hopeless, then at the last minute, he got another job and bought the bike on credit. Music rises, tears swell—bingo, a hit."

"Joey's Birthday," she said. "I saw it. I loved it. Heck, I even shed a tear or so myself. And it was funny in parts, too."

"If you can make people laugh, and cry, and end up feeling good, then you're on your way."

"So why did you give me all that baloney about high concept, and glitz?"

"That's what goes down at the meetings, babe," he said, with laughter glinting in his eyes. "I know you think I've gone Hollywood, but it's just an aberration. Every trade has its own style. As they say, miners don't wear white shirts. There's a lot of tension, and the jokes and jargon help ease it. I don't plan to act like this when I'm forty, you know. For me it's all new and glamorous. Heck, it's fun, but it's also a means to an end. You have to keep body and soul together while you're writing what you want to write. The networks like a sure thing, which means something that's succeeded in the past. But imitation is never really first-rate. The good stuff has to come from the heart."

"I have to write what the periodicals want. I've been try- ing to break into magazines," she explained.

"Write what you feel and worry about the marketplace after you have a first-rate piece down. You'll probably find they'll take something a little different, if it's good enough."

"You know, you could be a really nice guy, if you'd only be yourself."

"If my new show flies, I can even stop bleaching my hair and trying to look the part. Don't tell anybody, but it's a fictionalized play about Uncle Mike and Aunt Dora, and how you can lose your soul by running after the buck. That's been done a few thousand times, as well, but I have firsthand insights. That anniversary party—what a climax. The gold watch was so symbolic, but Mike really retired from his marriage about twenty years ago."

"I thought of that, too."

"Great minds think alike." He tapped her forehead. "Maybe there *is* a writer in there, trying to wiggle out. When you think you have something really good, send it to me, and I'll look at it. If I agree with you, I'll send it to my agent."

"Thanks, Matt. I want to go home and start writing right now."

"And I have to be getting to the airport, so let's split, babe."

Matt drove her home, and in the silence of the apart- ment, Donna thought about what he'd said. *Joey's Birth- day* reminded her of her own childhood. The time that stood out from all the rest was the summer her mother was sick. She'd been in the hospital for two weeks, and a terrified five- year-old Donna was scared stiff that she'd never come back.

The words seemed to jump onto the paper. She even felt a warm tear in her eye as she wrote. She was glad Cousin

Matt hadn't gone completely Hollywood. That facade was just assumed to help him get along with his colleagues. Like camouflage, to hide that underneath he was just plain folks.

Chapter Nine

The sun was a glowing red circle when Donna rose Monday morning. It was the kind of sun that set the sky on fire with its radiance. The thermometer read seventy-five degrees at 6:00 a.m., and the announcer on the radio threatened ninety-plus before evening.

Donna wore a sleeveless top to beat the heat, hoping that Adam would find some unstrenuous job for her that morning, one preferably indoors. The barn was surprisingly cool because of its cavernous size and the stand of maples shading it.

Donna smiled as she drove along the tree-shaded highway, admiring the grazing holsteins and the country quiet. It was already hot enough that the cows were seeking shade.

Adam wasn't around when she arrived, but Joe was there. Some of the calves she'd been bottle-feeding were drinking from the bucket now, and she had to measure out their milk carefully. Donna was finished with the feeding chores by eight, and went to ask Joe what she should do.

"You might as well get on with painting the fence out front," Joe said.

She got the paint and brush and went out front. What remained to be painted was in full sunlight. As the morning progressed, the temperature soared. Sweat poured from her forehead, and she knew her arms and shoulders would be red by evening. It seemed a long time till the ten o'clock coffee break. Adam wouldn't want her to continue in this heat, and she wouldn't argue. She'd put in more than a token half morning's work.

She was glad to see that Debbie had switched the refreshment from hot coffee to iced tea. Adam wasn't on the patio with the others, but Joe mentioned her sunburned arms and said, "That's enough painting for today, Donna. You're red as a lobster. We don't want you to get sunstroke."

Adam came out to the patio while they were talking. Donna turned to smile at him. He gave a curt nod to the whole group, not distinguishing her in any way. She thought he must be worried about something. He was carrying one of the reports that the government sent regularly. They often put him in a bad mood. He sat a little apart from the others, perusing the report.

Donna allowed herself the luxury of watching him while he read. His complexion had darkened noticeably over the summer. He was so still that he might have been a carved figure. Sturdy oak, strong and unyielding, seemed the proper medium to represent Adam. He had combed his jet-black hair severely into place. Donna felt an urge to run her fingers through it.

Her reverie was interrupted by Joe. "So, did you have a nice weekend, Donna?" he asked. She noticed the report jiggle in Adam's fingers.

"Yes, we had a family reunion Saturday night for Mike Calvert's twenty-fifth anniversary. My cousin was visiting from California. He writes for television." She turned to include Adam in the conversation, but he had resumed reading his report. "You may have heard of him, Matt Hibbert?"

"The name sounds familiar," Joe said. "He's not a Calvert then?"

"No, he's a cousin of Mike's wife, actually."

"Then he isn't really your cousin."

"Some relation," she said vaguely. "Maybe a cousin-in-law or something."

"Kissing cousin," Joe said vaguely.

"We've always considered him a cousin. He's very interesting. He was driving a Ferrari. I'd never been in one before."

"Wow! A Ferrari. I was in a Maserati once," Joe said. "At a car show. They didn't let you drive it, but you could sit inside."

"I didn't get to drive the Ferrari, either. But I got some good insights into writing. Matt said if I come up with a good script, he'd see about getting me an agent."

"Yup, it's not what you know, but who you know," Joe said.

From the corner of her eye, Donna sensed Adam's head turn to listen in. She was acutely aware that he was there, beside her, and wanted to talk to him, or at least exchange a smile. But when she looked his way, his eyes had returned to the report.

"I wouldn't say that. The work has to be good. Of course it helps to get it looked at if you know someone," she admitted.

"How long's this Matt fellow staying?" Joe asked.

"He left Sunday."

Adam didn't say a word, but he was having trouble keeping quiet. If he and Donna had been alone, she would have heard a few things. She couldn't be bothered with him when she had a bigger fish to fry, but as soon as this Matt person left, she was eager to continue researching him. It sounded as if she'd been putting her cousin to good use, as well.

When the break was nearly over, Joe turned to Adam and said, "Have you got any little chores indoors for Donna, Adam? She's getting sunburned from working in the sun."

Adam looked up from his report. His smoky eyes had turned to flint. They had a chilling effect as they glanced off her perspiring body. "You haven't dressed properly," he said. "Debbie will find a long-sleeved shirt for you. I'm anxious to get the fence finished."

Donna just stared in confusion. Why was he acting like this? She had objected to special treatment, but that didn't mean she wanted to be parboiled.

"Couldn't that wait for a cooler day?" Joe asked doubtfully. "One of us has to drive over to the co-op store."

"I'm doing that myself," Adam said. "Donna wants to earn her wage." He just glanced at her. "Or do you feel you can't handle the job?" There was a challenge in his tone.

Joe opened his lips to object, but Donna got in before him. "That's all right, Joe. I don't mind."

"That's what I'm paying her for," Adam said, directing his words to Joe, but very much aware that Donna was looking askance at him. She wanted to learn about a farmer's life, then let her. It wasn't an easy one. Adam set the report on the table, rose and went directly to his van without even saying goodbye.

"What ails him?" Joe asked.

Donna hunched her burning shoulders. "Beats me. Has he had some bad news or something?" She looked at the report.

"He hasn't shared it with me if he has." Joe picked up the report and glanced at it. "This is a month old. He's been like a bear all weekend. I stopped by for a swim yesterday afternoon. He didn't have a friendly word to say."

"He was here?" she asked, frowning. "He told me he had to go out of town."

"Maybe he went in the morning. He didn't say. Didn't say boo the whole time I was here. He mustn't realize how hot it is in the sun, Donna. You leave the painting for some day it's cooler. I'll show you how to mix the feed this morning. It'd be a good thing for you to know."

"No, I'd better do what Adam wants," she said.

"All right. But be sure you cover your shoulders." Joe went to the kitchen door and asked Debbie for a long-sleeved white shirt. "An old one. It might get paint stains."

Debbie brought one of Adam's old shirts. Donna felt strange, wearing his shirt. She was afraid something was bothering Adam, and hoped it wasn't serious. The shirt helped, but it was still uncomfortably hot working in the sun. She kept an eye out for the returning wagon, thinking Adam would stop, but at eleven-thirty when it zoomed up the road, raising a dust cloud, he didn't even glance at her.

Two more days continued in the same hostile way. Donna attempted a few friendly remarks, but got no response. Adam assigned her harder, heavier work such as getting in the hay and cleaning out the stalls. Manure removal was done mechanically, but he had her hose down the stalls and sweep the barn. Adam didn't take coffee break with the others after the first day. On the few occasions when he spoke to Donna at all, he was stiff and businesslike, more so than with the other employees. But what confirmed that his mood was more than some general malaise was that he didn't ask her out again.

Donna was deeply engrossed in her writing, but she still wanted to know why he'd changed. Was it something she'd done? She racked her mind, but couldn't think of anything.

When she discussed it with her cousin, Jeanie said, "Why don't you just ask him?"

"He seems so angry, I'm half afraid to."

"Don't be silly. Don't you think he'd ask you, if the shoe were on the other foot? Wouldn't you want him to? From what you say, it sounds as if his feelings have gotten hurt. Well, tell him he's hurting your feelings, too."

"Yeah, you're right. I've got to confront him." She determined to ask him point-blank at the first opportunity.

He used to make a point to be around when she arrived in the morning. Donna didn't think it was by chance that he wasn't around these days.

"Where's Adam, Joe?" she asked the next morning.

"You don't want to see him," he said, shaking his head. "I think I've figured out what's bugging him. He had a visit from Mike Calvert and some other feller yesterday afternoon. Mike wanted to buy the log cabin where Adam was born. I'll tell you, the air was blue. Mike and his friend skedaddled out of here pretty fast."

"I told Mac that Adam would never go for that."

"The fellow must have given Adam the wrong idea. I was here when they came. I heard your name mentioned."

"I suppose that could be it, but it isn't my fault. And Adam seemed cool before yesterday."

"I thought maybe you two had had a little tiff," Joe said, looking for her reaction.

"No, we haven't. That's what's so weird about it. Does he take these fits of temper often?"

"Never before, as far as I can remember. Oh, he has a temper for anyone who tries to take advantage of him, but you wouldn't do that."

"No, I haven't done anything. Maybe Mac phoned him Monday, and Adam's been brooding about this all week, thinking I had something to do with it."

"Why don't you have a word with him before you feed the calves? He's in his office. He's getting impossible to work with. Like a caged lion, snarling and thrashing his tail."

"Maybe you're right. I'll go before I get all hot and dirty."

She went reluctantly to the kitchen, and Debbie let her in. "I'd like to speak to Adam," Donna said.

"He's in his study, chewing nails and slamming drawers," Debbie said crossly. His bad mood was putting everyone out of sorts. "He told me the coffee was cold. Cold! And I just took it off the stove."

Donna's flagging confidence fell a notch to hear that Adam was in a bad mood, but she wanted to get this settled once and for all, so she went to his office and tapped at the door.

"What is it?" a curt voice called.

As she had no intention of discussing this personal matter through the closed door, she opened it and stepped in. In the few seconds when she caught him off guard, she thought that Adam didn't look very angry. No, he looked unhappy. His expression wasn't the harsh one she had been seeing; he wore a softer, troubled look. She felt a rush of sympathy and went toward him. "Adam, what's the matter?" she asked impulsively.

His face froze in displeasure, and when he spoke, his voice was like an Arctic blast. "The only thing I see the matter is that it's nearly seven o'clock and you're not feeding the calves."

It was hard to press on in the face of his monumental indifference, but she continued. "You seem so cold. If it's about Uncle Mike, I want you to know I didn't put him up to trying to buy the log cabin. I told Mac you wouldn't go for it."

"Then you *were* aware of the scheme and didn't bother mentioning to me that it was your uncle's idea."

"It didn't seem my place to interfere in your business, and besides, we've hardly exchanged two words all week."

"You're right. You're hired as a stable hand, Donna," he said coolly. "I don't expect you to concern yourself with my business affairs. You may be sure I won't let Mike Calvert set up a shop on my property."

His arrogance strained her nerves, and when she replied, her voice was louder. "You said yourself you have space to spare, and it would make a good rent. That sounds like cutting off your nose to spite your face."

"I didn't say a shop wouldn't be opened. I just said it wouldn't be Mike Calvert who did it. Sorry to interfere with your plans."

Her annoyance firmed to anger. "They weren't *my* plans. It's irrelevant to me if you let stupid pride get in the way of profit. I just wanted you to know I had nothing to do with it, if that's why you've been acting like a bear all week. Making me paint in the sweltering sun..." She hadn't meant to complain and stopped short.

"I told you in the beginning I usually hired men. If you find the work's too much for you, don't feel obliged to stay."

"No! I can handle the work. It's not that."

He looked at her as if she were a troublesome stranger. "Then what seems to be the problem?" he asked.

This was really too much. She put her hands on her hips and lit into him. "The problem, among other things, is that you told me you had to go out of town last Sunday, but you were right here all the time."

"What's sauce for the goose... You told me you were attending a family reunion."

"I was!"

"I offered to go with you."

"You would have hated it."

"But you and your kissing cousin didn't hate it, did you, babe?"

She stood, no longer glaring, but staring when she heard that telltale word. It almost sounded as if Adam had been there... How did he know about *babe?* But everyone was using that stupid expression now. It was on TV all the time.

"I don't really consider Matt Hibbert a kissing cousin," she said.

"He isn't a *cousin* at all, so far as I can figure out. But then a man doesn't really have to be a cousin to be useful, does he?"

"I don't see anything wrong with asking him for a little advice. That's all it was."

"And what about *me?*" he demanded, his voice rising as his temper flared. "What was my role, Donna? To provide a caricature for your farm epic? Pa Kettle, with the seat out of his pants and hayseeds in his hair?"

Babe and Pa Kettle—that was too much of a coincidence. "You were there!" she charged.

"Yes, like a fool, I was there, thinking I might catch you as you returned Saturday night. I wish to hell I hadn't been."

She heard the echo of pain in his tirade and tried to remember what they had been talking about. Pa Kettle, obviously, but she hadn't said anything to make fun of Adam. "We were just laughing and joking around," she said. "I wasn't making fun of you, if that's what you think."

"It sounded mighty like it, babe. And the boots were not a present. They were merely part of your work tools, since you neglected my suggestion that you provide a pair for yourself."

Her temper soared at his offensive tone. "I think it was despicable of you to spy on me! Why didn't you come out of the bushes and let me know you were there, if you were waiting for me?" she charged.

"I wasn't in the bushes. I was in my car, but you were too engrossed to notice. You were all having such a merry old time at my expense I didn't want to interrupt your party, so I left. We farmers keep early hours." He glanced at the clock with an air of impatience. "Speaking of hours, it's time you got to work."

"People who eavesdrop shouldn't complain if they hear something they don't like," she retorted angrily.

"I'm not complaining, just explaining. You asked what was wrong. I'm telling you. If you feel you've finished your research here, don't feel obliged to stick around. I can always find a replacement."

"Are you telling me I'm fired?" she demanded, hardly able to believe he'd go this far.

"You seem to have trouble understanding basic English—not a very promising sign for someone who claims to be an author. I said if you want to leave, don't feel you have to stay."

She still couldn't make out exactly what was expected of her, but she knew at least that Adam wouldn't lift a finger to keep her here. She stood a moment, undecided, then turned and walked out without notifying him one way or the other.

She blinked back angry tears as she struggled into her boots and returned to the barn. Joe was busy with the milking, which gave her a few minutes to collect her thoughts. It wouldn't be fair if she left now, Joe would have to do the feeding on top of all his other chores. So she'd finish out the week, only today and tomorrow. They had weekend help, so there would be a few days to replace her.

She filled the buckets and held the bottles for the younger calves, looking at the big-eyed, glossy animals as they drank. She knew them all by name now, knew all their little quirks and tricks. Brigitte always tried to lick her hand. Yvette's tail kept switching all the time she drank. Mimi didn't like Brigitte. She couldn't feed the pair at the same time. She'd miss the calves.

Her heart twisted in disappointment. She would miss everything about this job. She loved the drive to work in the quiet morning. It was a period for contemplation. Driving home gave her time to switch mental gears from the farm to the supermarket, and to prepare herself for the hassle of the cash register and customers. She could probably get hired full-time at the supermarket since she couldn't live on half-days' pay, but preferred work at the farm.

She was just finishing up when Joe joined her. It was time to lead the cattle to the pasture, and she'd always helped him with this chore.

"How'd it go?" he asked.

"Awful!" she said, her shoulders sagging.

Joe looked as if he'd like to ask more, but leading the cows out was a demanding job. He just moved on, pressing the cows into line. When they were in the pasture and the gate was closed, he said, "Do you want to talk about it? You look kind of weary, Donna. A shoulder to cry on..."

"It's all a stupid misunderstanding. Adam was waiting for me outside my apartment building Saturday night. He heard me talking to Matt and the others. They were just joking about me being a farmer. Just silly things, but Adam thought we were—thought I was laughing at him. I'd never do that. I love—I love it here. I'll miss all this so much."

She looked out at the peacefully grazing cows. The field of black and white and green blurred as tears sprang into her eyes. She wiped them away with the back of her hand. "I'll be leaving on Friday for good, Joe. I hope that gives you time to find a replacement."

"Oh, no! Gee, Donna, I wish you'd think it over."

"He practically fired me," she said angrily. "I don't have to beg for a job like this."

"Adam has a short fuse, but he gets over his tempers quickly. It's that French streak. His mother's the same way. Why don't you think it over?"

"There's nothing to think about. I feel as if I'm working in a deep freeze when Adam's around." Joe couldn't argue with that. "Now, what do you want me to do this morning?" she asked, switching to business.

"Time to cut the grass again. You know how to use the lawn tractor now."

"Is it in the garage?"

"Yup."

Donna smiled when she noticed what he'd said. It wasn't Adam who said that, after all, it was *Joe*. If she was going to get background for a farmer from this job, it was Joe she would use as a model, not Adam. Adam was more businessman than farmer.

The weather had returned to normal. Mowing on the tractor was a pleasant job, so Donna didn't bother with her coffee break. She could get it all done by noon if she didn't stop. Besides, she wasn't exactly eager to share the patio with Adam.

When Joe noticed Adam looking around for Donna at coffee break, he said, "She's mowing the lawn. Probably doesn't realize the time. Someone ought to tell her."

Adam didn't have to ask who "she" was. "She has a watch," he said with an air of indifference.

"Yup. Should I call her?"

"No, she'll come when she's ready."

"Coffee'll be gone by then." Adam didn't answer. "She's quitting," Joe said, and looked for a reaction. Adam's jaw didn't drop as he hoped, but it clenched tighter. "Gave her notice. Won't be back on Monday."

"That's pretty short notice," he said with a scowl. "It's about what I expected."

"You must have chewed her out pretty good," Joe said accusingly.

"I don't care to talk about it, Joe."

Joe ignored this. "She wasn't too happy about it. I think you could talk her into staying, if you'd apologize."

"I have nothing to apologize for."

"She wasn't making fun of you, Adam. Said she'd never do that."

"What the hell did she do, run and cry on your shoulder?"

"No, she was just sort of sniffling into her hand. I felt so sad I darn near bawled myself."

"Don't be a fool," Adam said. He picked up his coffee. "Tell her it's time for coffee break," he said, then he strode angrily into his office, feeling like a hardened monster.

It was the image evoked by Donna sniffling into her hand that had done it. He'd been too hard on her. But soon other images were superimposed on the endearing one. Donna arriving in that Italian sports car with the blond guy who was not her cousin. Laughing at him. Let her go. The longer this went on, the more he was going to get hurt.

He had absolutely nothing in common with any woman who could sing the praises of that phony Hollywood producer. He couldn't find much to admire in her cousin's Yuppie tennis-playing friend, either. They just weren't his kind of people. Maybe he'd become narrow-minded, living on the farm, but he knew insincerity when he saw it. Except when he saw it in Donna. She had fooled him once before. Sniffling into her hand wasn't going to fool him this time.

Adam didn't know until after twelve whether Donna had taken her coffee break or not. He couldn't see the patio from his office, and he was too proud to go out and look. But when he saw the lawn all mowed after she left, he knew she hadn't. What was she trying to do, impress him with how hard she worked?

She took her coffee break the next morning, but she sat with her back to Adam, talking in a low voice to Joe. Adam pretended he was reading the paper. When the break was over, she said, "That's a good idea, Joe. I'll think about it. Thanks for the tip." Then she left, without speaking to Adam.

"What was that all about?" Adam asked.

"I told Donna Mrs. McAllister might hire her. She's got twenty-four students now. Donna rides. Took lessons back home."

"That won't work. Mrs. McAllister wants someone for the afternoon students. I doubt Donna really needs the money," he said.

"You're wrong there. She's worried sick. She thought the supermarket would take her full-time, but they're all full up."

After a moment, Adam said, "Have you found anyone to replace her?"

"Nope. I've got ads in the papers. I let the employment office know. Haven't had a single bid." Joe crossed his fingers. He had two names and phone numbers from the employment agency.

"Tell her she's welcome to stay on, if she really needs the money."

"Why don't *you* tell her? You're the one who fired her."

"I didn't fire her!"

"Whatever you said, Adam, she's not going to stay on unless you apologize to her."

"I'll be damned if I'll apologize. She's the one who should apologize."

Joe just shook his head. Stubborn as a mule. "Don't forget to include her earned holiday pay. She'll need the money," he said, and walked away.

The employees went to Adam's office to collect their pay on Friday at noon. If he was away, he left the checks with Debbie. Donna hoped he had done that today. She didn't know how to say goodbye to Adam. She noticed his wagon was parked under the trees when she went to the house, and knew Adam was there. She waited until the two other part-timers came before going inside.

"He's in his office," Debbie said, over her shoulder. "I hope you've all taken off those boots. I washed the floor today."

No one dared to enter Debbie's kitchen without first removing their boots. The three employees went to Adam's door. It was open.

Adam looked up from his computer. "Pay day, folks," he smiled, picking up the checks. It was a strained, unnatural smile. It didn't touch his eyes, but it was the first smile Donna had seen in a week, and she found herself turning a little soft inside.

Adam handed the men their checks first, then waited a moment. "How about me?" she asked.

"I'd like a word with you, Donna. Can you wait a minute?"

"Sure." She was wildly curious to know what he might say. She waited while the others got their pay and left. "What is it?" she asked, determined to be all business.

"Have you found other work?" he asked. "Joe mentioned the riding stable."

"I plan to run up there before I leave."

"You realize it's afternoon help Mrs. McAllister needs?"

"Afternoons! Oh, that's when I work at the supermarket."

"I know. If you want to stay on for the time being, we'd be glad to have you. It's tough finding help this time of year," he added, to ease his pride.

"You'll easily find someone," she said. "Was that all, Adam?"

"I guess so... thank you, Donna. You were a good worker. I'm sorry to be losing you."

A good worker! As if that's all there had ever been between them. "And I'll miss the cows," she said glibly. "Are you going to give me that check, or is it glued to your hand?"

He handed it over. "Feel free to come back and visit the cows anytime."

"I prefer a clean break, Adam," she said, staring boldly to let him know what she thought of his shilly-shallying way of getting rid of her. He met her gaze without wavering. She felt herself being drawn into the depths of those crystal eyes, and looked at her check, as an excuse to divert her eyes. "This is too much!"

"I've included your earned vacation pay. It's standard business practice."

"Oh. Well, I guess this is goodbye, then, Adam. I enjoyed working here."

"I enjoyed having you work here. Good luck on your job hunting, and on your writing."

"Thanks. I'll need it."

She turned and hurried out of the office in her stocking feet. She wished she was wearing shoes, so that she could click her heels in disdain.

She said goodbye to Debbie, who seemed genuinely sorry to see her go. Joe came to the van to say a final farewell, and she was off. It was the first time she didn't enjoy the drive home. The cattle in the pastures were a sad reminder of what she was leaving behind.

Chapter Ten

"It's the Capricorn thing," Jeanie said as she set the table for dinner that evening. Donna was telling her the story of her day. "I warned you air and earth signs are a poor mix. Capricorns are not only headstrong and unyielding, they have very strong likes and dislikes."

"Especially dislikes," Donna said as she sprinkled parsley on the stir-fry she was preparing.

"You Geminis are apt to misplace your confidence," Jeanie explained. "You're too susceptible to kindness."

"It's not his kindness that troubles me. It's his unkindness."

"He offered to let you stay on, though," Jeanie reminded her.

"Oh, big deal! Was I supposed to get on my hands and knees for that? If I have to beg for a job, I'd rather beg at the supermarket."

"But he did offer. That's a major concession for a Capricorn, Donna. I think he still likes you. Capricorns are good at overcoming obstacles. Maybe he'll think up some other way to get you back. They'll go to great extremes to get what they want."

"He didn't have to go to any great extreme. All he had to do was apologize. Dinner is ready. Let's eat."

She served the food and they began eating.

Donna said, "Did Mac mention anything about the tack shop at Samara? You knew Adam put the kibosh on it?"

"Yeah, he said Adam was really mad. That's because Uncle Mike wanted to buy the log cabin, after Adam told him the best he could hope for was to rent it. And it was a really low offer, too. You know how Mike loves to haggle. He never listens to anything but the tinkle of the cash register. He knows land always appreciates. Why pay rent for the shop when he could buy it? He would have paid a lot more than his first offer, of course, if Adam hadn't more or less kicked him out."

"I guess he'll open up the tack shop somewhere else. Hey, maybe I could get a job clerking in it. I know something about riding equipment."

"But it won't open for a few months," Jeanie pointed out. "And since we want to move upstairs, out of this dark apartment as soon as possible, you'll want a job right away."

"I'll find something," Donna said. "I'll tour the mall tomorrow, leave applications at all the chain stores. Something's bound to come up."

"Worst-case scenario," Jeanie said. "You can always hit Uncle Mike for a job."

"Worst-case scenario?" Donna said. "That sounds like Mac. You've been seeing too much of Mac."

"Not anymore. I told him last night it was over. Kaput. Finis. I couldn't stand hearing myself called babe any longer. Besides, I finally got a tumble from the cute Virgo who does the entertainment column on the *Beacon*. Doug Warwick. Thoughtful and romantic, red hair, freckles.''

"I didn't know the horoscope foretold hair color.''

"It doesn't really. Doug's taking me to a movie tonight. The paper pays. But about working at the *Beacon*, Mike's running a series of special articles on the history of the area. You know, landmarks, the early days, stuff like that. The vicar of the Anglican church is doing one on the building of St. Peter's. And the guy who renovated the old mill into a restaurant is doing one on the mill. Mike mentioned that somebody should do one about Samara.''

"I'm surprised he would, after his set-to with Adam,'' Donna exclaimed.

"He wouldn't let that interfere with the paper. Samara's a famous local landmark. It'd offend the historical society and the whole farming community if he didn't include Samara. Besides, Mike has kind of a soft spot for that area north of town. It's where he and our dads were born, you know. Mike mentioned you might like to take a stab at the Samara article, since you've worked there. He didn't want to ask Adam.''

"Adam would never do it, and I don't know enough about the history of the place to tackle it. But his mother might be interested,'' Donna said. "She has some great stories about the early days when she came to America as a war bride.''

"It'd make a great excuse for you to see Adam again,'' Jeanie said, with a conspiratorial smile.

"I've seen quite enough of him.''

"I'll mention to Mike that Mrs. Challow might do it, then. What are you doing tonight, Donna?''

"I'll be writing.''

"Don't you mean editing? You've finished the story about your mom being sick. I thought it was great, by the way. I cried.''

"It is finished, but now I have to put it aside for a while and read it with a fresh eye later. I'm starting another story."

"What about?"

"I don't know yet."

Donna thought about that while she cleared the table and washed the dishes. It wasn't her turn, but since Jeanie had an early date, they switched. Thoughts of Adam and the farm kept intruding. It would be fun to write that historical article for the *Beacon,* but she had no intention of doing it. It would look as if she were just making an excuse to go back. Besides, Adam probably wouldn't even want her there, talking to his mother. She wrote a letter to her own mother instead, since she was feeling nostalgic that night.

In the morning she made the rounds of the shops at the mall. The whole atmosphere seemed unreal. The piped-in music, the unnatural greenish-yellow light, the dry air. Of course, it was Samara she was missing. If she were there, she'd be outdoors now, her feeding chores done. Joe had mentioned teaching her to drive the real tractor, not the little one used for the lawn. She had been looking forward to it.

She had a sandwich at the mall and went to the supermarket in the afternoon. As usual, it was too busy to think there, which was a blessing in a way, since her mind always harped on the same sad thoughts.

Jeanie had gotten home before her. She was making Spanish omelettes and a salad for dinner. "What's shaking?" she asked, looking up from the stove.

"Not much. How was your day?"

"Busy. I got two new accounts. I have some news for you, too. Mike definitely wants you to do the Samara article."

"I told you I'm not interested," Donna said, rather sharply. It wasn't Mike or Jeanie she was angry with, but herself, for wanting to give in to temptation.

"Are you sure? The pay's good." She mentioned the rate, which was about twice what Donna had thought it would be.

"I'm positive. The camera shop might hire me. They're looking for someone for evenings."

"You don't know anything about cameras."

"I can learn."

"You don't want to work nights. What'll you do about dates?"

"What dates? Evenings suit me fine. I'd have the mornings for my writing, while I'm fresh."

"So you're definitely not interested in the article?"

"One hundred percent sure. That smells good. I'm going to wash up." She escaped to the washroom before she succumbed to temptation.

Jeanie had another date with her Virgo. He was taking her to a local dramatic presentation, also for free. Donna went to her typewriter, but her imagination seemed to have dried up. She didn't even think about trying a screenplay. She had admitted to herself that she wasn't comfortable with that choppy style of writing. What she really wanted to write was that article on Samara.

She would begin it with Mrs. Challow's surprising exclamation, *"Quel désastre!"* and go on to compare her first impression forty-five years ago with the prosperous and beautiful farm Samara was today. Adam would know the details about the herd. He had mentioned a good breeding cow could sell for upward of a million dollars.

When Jeanie returned at eleven o'clock, Donna had written a two-page eulogy about Samara as she knew it.

"What are you writing?" Jeanie asked.

She hastily shoved the two sheets under a blank sheet and said, "Just thinking. How was the play?"

They had a cup of tea and chatted before going to bed. The weekend seemed long and lonesome. Jeanie insisted that Donna join her and Doug for a picnic on Sunday. They went to Elbow Island. Donna kept watching the river for signs of Adam's boat, but it didn't come.

Late on Monday afternoon Donna looked up from her cash register at the supermarket to see Mrs. Challow placing a few parcels on the counter. She was surprised, as Debbie usually did the shopping.

"We miss you at Samara, Donna," Mrs. Challow said.

"I miss you, too." Donna smiled a noncommittal smile as she drew a bag of rice over the code bar reader. "How are the cows?"

"Lonesome. They have feelings, too."

"I hope it doesn't put them off their feed."

"No, the *cows* are eating as much as usual," she said. Her flashing brown eyes suggested that someone at Samara was not, and that someone was Adam.

"That'll be seven fifty-five," Donna said, hastily shoving the groceries into a bag.

"You finish at six, I think?" Mrs. Challow said.

"Yes, in five minutes." Now what was all this about? Donna had the absurd idea that Adam was waiting in the wagon.

"I'm alone today," Mrs. Challow said. "Adam had to go to Albany on some government business. I was wondering if you'd have dinner with me. Here, in the mall. It is dull eating alone. Or do you have plans for dinner?"

"No." Eating with Mrs. Challow was about the last thing in the world Donna wanted, but she was so stunned that she couldn't come up with an excuse on the spur of the moment.

"Good. I'll be waiting for you in Galliger's Restaurant." Mrs. Challow picked up her bag and hurried out.

Galliger's was a fancy spot. Donna knew she'd look completely out of place. Since she had to wear a uniform at work, she didn't bother dressing up, and today she'd worn jeans and a blouse. She tidied herself up as best as she could after work, but she still felt underdressed in the dimly lit restaurant. At least it wasn't busy. Most diners didn't arrive before eight, although it opened at six.

Mrs. Challow sat at a table for two near the door. She was sipping a glass of wine and glancing at the menu.

The waiter cast one imperious look at Donna's jeans. She said, "Mrs. Challow's table, please," and followed him down the aisle.

"I've ordered us white wine," Mrs. Challow said, smiling at her. "It's not very good, I'm afraid. So kind of you to come, Donna, and so foolish of me to give you no notice."

"I feel out of place in jeans."

Mrs. Challow didn't seem bothered. "One sees jeans everywhere nowadays. I wish I could wear them, but I am too wide in the derriere. Now, you must be wondering why I am really here." Donna's heart lurched, and she looked around for Adam. What else could it be? "No, not that!" Mrs. Challow said, and laughed archly. "He really is in Albany. I am here about something else. We had the most astonishing visit from your uncle this morning, before Adam left."

"Oh, no!" Donna exclaimed. "Don't tell me he's pestering Adam again about that tack shop."

"No, that is what Adam thought, too. He was quite angry, but it was me Mr. Calvert wished to speak to. His paper is doing a series of historical sketches of the area, and of course he wants to include Samara. He says someone suggested to him that I might be interested."

"Oh, dear, I guess that's my fault. I mentioned to my cousin that you knew more about it than anyone else, but I never thought he'd approach you in person."

"But I am thrilled!" Mrs. Challow said. "I agreed at once. In fact, I spent the whole day slaving over Adam's word processor. I have done a rough draft. The reason I called on you was that I thought you might have a look at what I have written, as you are a writer."

"I see," Donna said, stunned. She picked up her wineglass and sipped the cool liquid. It felt good after her busy afternoon. Mrs. Challow ordered lobster. "My treat," she said, when she saw Donna's eyes running across the menu to check the prices.

"Then I'll have the same. I love lobster," Donna said. She knew she wasn't being entirely polite, but she liked lobster too much to pass it up.

"That will be two lobsters," Mrs. Challow informed the waiter.

After they had chosen their side dishes and the waiter had left, Donna said, "About proofreading your article, they do have editors at the *Beacon*, Mrs. Challow."

"Call me Honoré."

"And not Renée?" Donna said impishly.

"No, Honoré is more serious, for a writer. I know they have editors, but they are grammarians," she said dismissively. "I am not interested in commas and apostrophes. I want you to tell me if the article is artistic, literary. I want to do Samara justice."

"I'd be very happy to read it."

Mrs. Challow opened her purse and handed Donna two typed pages. "You can take it home and study it. We shouldn't interrupt our lobster with work. I enjoyed writing this article very much. I am thinking of composing a poem next. Perhaps something in free verse."

"About Samara?" Donna asked, trying not to look shocked at this sudden foray into the world of literature.

"Love is the only subject for a *française*. I leave nature to the English poets. That is all they're good for."

Donna took exception. "Some of the best love poems were written by the English. Byron, Keats, Shelley—the whole romantic school."

"Ah, but have you read Villon?"

"That was a long time ago! The fifteenth century."

"He has never been surpassed. And he died so young, only in his thirties."

"All the English romantics died young, Keats was only in his twenties."

They discussed literature over their lobster. Mrs. Challow was interested, and seemed somewhat surprised at Donna's extensive knowledge.

"I studied it at college," Donna explained.

When dessert was served, Mrs. Challow adroitly changed the topic to more personal matters. She liked what she had seen of Donna Calvert. She was a spirited, intelligent girl. By the time they had had coffee she had confirmed that she was hardworking and conscientious. So why had she gone darting off from her job, leaving them shorthanded? Obviously that son of hers had done something idiotic. But Adam was not a complete idiot, so he must have offended Donna inadvertently. Being a Frenchwoman, Mrs. Challow assumed the offense was of a romantic nature.

She decided she would learn the details from her son. "I'll drive you home now," she said, when the bill was paid and they were preparing to leave.

Before Donna left the car, Mrs. Challow said, "Can I call you tomorrow about the article? Or will you have time to look at it tonight?"

"I plan to read it as soon as I get home."

"Not going out?" she asked with a sharp eye.

"Not tonight."

"Then I'll call you tomorrow morning. I appreciate your taking the time to do this for me."

"I'm sure it'll be a pleasure. And thanks for the great dinner, Mrs. Challow."

"I enjoyed your company, Donna. We'll do it again."

Donna was extremely curious to see what Mrs. Challow had written. She darted straight to the sofa and arranged the lamp over her shoulder. After ten minutes, she set the two sheets aside and frowned. Was this really Mrs. Challow's idea of a literary effort? It read like something out of an encyclopedia, all dates and dull facts and no feeling. She could hardly believe the effervescent Mrs. Challow had written it.

If Mike was eager enough to include Samara in his series, he'd have someone at the paper do a rewrite. Otherwise, he'd just return it to Mrs. Challow and increase the hard feelings between the two families. She didn't want to hurt Mrs. Challow's feelings, but there was no point telling her that her writing was good, or even acceptable, because it wasn't.

She was still brooding over the problem when Mrs. Challow phoned at nine the next morning. "Would it be convenient for me to come now?" she asked.

"Yes, the sooner, the better. I have to be at work at two."

"I'll be right there."

Donna spent the interval tidying up herself and the apartment. Mrs. Challow was too polite to stare, but she was surprised to find herself being shown into a small basement apartment.

"Coffee?" Donna offered.

"That would be lovely, dear." Donna got the coffee and joined Mrs. Challow on the sofa. Mrs. Challow saw her reluctance to speak and said, "I think Victor Hugo does not have to worry, eh?"

"It's very interesting," Donna said. "All those facts. I was surprised at how little your husband paid for the farm."

"Money was worth more in those days."

"Yes."

"Now tell me the bad news," Mrs. Challow said with a wry grin.

"The article doesn't seem to—I mean I didn't get any— it's sort of dry," she finally blurted out. "When you talked to me about those old days, it was all so interesting, but you left all the good stuff out of your article. How you cried and wanted to go back to Paris. And how cold the first winter was in the log cabin. How you stuffed rags and paper between the boards, like a real pioneer."

"Writing is very hard," Mrs. Challow said. "It took a whole day to write those two pages. My head ached when I was finished. I had to use the dictionary at every sentence. It is the language problem, you see. I speak English, but I haven't had much occasion to write it. I write my letters home in French. I read many French books and magazines, as well. Adam scolds me for it."

"I suggest you give these sheets to Mike, and he'll have one of his writers pad the article out. The writer will probably want to interview you."

"You are not working in the mornings?" Mrs. Challow asked.

"No, I'm still looking for work."

"Meanwhile, would you be interested . . ."

Donna was torn between a rampant desire to do the article, and an equally strong wish to have nothing to do with Samara and Adam.

"No reporter knows the farm as well as you do," Mrs. Challow said persuasively. "You have the feel, the rhythm of it. You know how hard the work is, and how satisfying the rewards. Not to mention your financial reward for doing the article," she added.

This last speech reminded Donna that this was just a job. The first professional one she'd been offered. It was too good to refuse. "I'll give it a try. We'll split the fee fifty-fifty. Okay?"

Mrs. Challow finished her coffee and rose. "I just assembled those facts from deeds and documents. Mike gave me an idea what sort of information he wanted. I can hardly call that writing. I would have done the same, gratis, for whoever wrote the article. I tried myself, but the words stuck in my brain and refused to come out. So we'll call it research. The money is not important to me, Donna. My payment will be reading the article. I'll send copies home to my family."

"It doesn't seem quite fair," Donna said.

"Then you can buy me lunch some day."

"All right, you've got a deal."

"Now I'll let you get at it."

She left, and Donna dashed to the typewriter. She collected her own earlier jottings and Mrs. Challow's facts, and began work. It was the most enjoyable writing she had ever done. Putting herself inside another person's head and mentally living her life—maybe that was the secret of writing fiction? It was fun transforming Mrs. Challow to a young Parisienne and transplanting her to what was then a derelict farm with a primitive log cabin. Of course Mrs. Challow was not a stranger to hardship, as she had survived the war in France. That was probably what had made the transition possible.

Donna thought about it all the time she was at work the next day and resumed writing that evening. By the next evening, she was satisfied that she had done her best and called Mrs. Challow.

"The opus is finished. Want to have a look at it before I take it to the *Beacon?*"

"I'd love to. Can I pick it up tomorrow afternoon?"

"But you know I work afternoons. I'll take it to the store. Is that okay?"

"That's fine. I'm looking forward to it."

It was Joe who picked the article up. Donna was busy and didn't have much time to talk to him.

"How're you doing, Donna?" he asked.

"Fine. Did you get someone to replace me at the farm?"

"Yeah, we got a first-year psychology student. He's been creating havoc, feeding the cows we're trying to dry out and leaving gates open and spilling milk. He tells us Brigitte has an inferiority complex. I kind of wish Rambo was still around."

"Maybe I didn't do so badly for a beginner."

"We miss you," Joe said. Donna looked up, wondering about that "we." Did he mean Adam?

"How's Adam?" she asked.

"He's settled back to normal." And she was so busy, Joe took the envelope and left.

Donna thought about what he had said. Adam had settled back to normal, forgotten all about her in other words. She thoughtlessly rammed a can of peas on top of a bag of grapes.

"Watch what you're doing!" the customer complained.

"Sorry," Donna said, and removed the can.

That evening, Mrs. Challow gave Adam the article to read. He read it through quickly to get an idea of Donna's writing style, then read it more slowly, savoring the flavor of it. Her love of Samara was evident in every line. He had often admired the sunrise himself, the way the morning sky brightened from white to streaks of lemon and peach and orange, as the sun rose over the maples. She described the whisper of the wind in the trees, and the silver mist that blew like smoke over the pasture on rainy days. It felt eerie to see his own vague thoughts put into words, as if he and Donna were a part of the same psyche.

But it was one sentence that he kept returning to. She was writing about the long hours, the risks and the physical labor involved. "It's a hard life, and it takes a hard man to farm successfully." A hard man. Was that how she saw him? A man without feelings? Didn't she have any idea how much he was hurting?

"What do you think?" his mother asked.

His thoughts were too private to discuss. "There isn't much here about the business end of the operation," he said. "The record-breaking yield we get, and where we sell our cows. The breeding farm is hardly mentioned, except for Rambo."

"Why don't you jot down the statistics, and she can add a couple of paragraphs at the end?"

"I'll do that. Joe can take it to her tomorrow," he said.

"I thought it was a lovely article. I had no idea Donna appreciated Samara so much," she said. "And she writes so well! I wonder why she can't sell her other pieces. It seems a shame she has to pack groceries, when she has a talent like this. And living in that shabby little basement apartment! Mike should do something for her."

"I'll jot down those figures while I have a minute free," Adam said, and went to his office to think in private.

He looked at the article again. Any idea that Donna had been making fun of farming or of himself was removed by the glowing praise he read here. "A hard man." He had earned that description, sending her out in the boiling sun to paint. He had regretted it a hundred times. How could he show her he wasn't made of granite, but of flesh and blood? He obviously had to apologize, and ask her to come back. He jotted down the information he felt should be included and went to the wagon to drive into Bayville.

Donna was annoyed to have her work interrupted when the buzzer sounded at eight-thirty. "Who is it?" she called through the intercom.

"It's Adam," he said, and tensed for a sharp rebuke. There was a noticeable silence. "It's about the article," he added, to ensure being let in.

"All right." The buzzer sounded, and he hurried to get in the outer door while it was unlocked.

He looked around for her apartment, recalling his mother's words about "a shabby little basement apartment." Her statement hadn't registered then. He had to go down a dark and narrow stairway with a dim light at the bottom. The marble and chandelier of the foyer had changed to linoleum and rough plaster painted a sickly beige. There was a noticeable aroma from the incinerator. He hated to think of Donna living here, but when she opened the door, he noticed that she had tried to liven up the place.

The unexpected call hadn't left Donna time to primp. Her dark hair was in a tousle, held back with a yellow scarf. Without makeup, she looked pale. But it was the mutinous set of her lips that worried him.

"What did you think of the article?" she asked. Her chin was up, ready for a battle.

"It was great. Mom loved it." She still seemed to be waiting. "So did I."

She relaxed a bit. "Good. But you didn't have to return it. That's only a carbon copy."

"Actually I wanted to make a few additions." When she cast a suspicious glance, he hurried on. "About the business end of the operation. The fact that we sell cows to Europe and recently Asia is interesting. I've jotted down a few sales and prices. The yield per cow, and so on. No reason you should have known that, and Mom didn't think to include it."

He handed her the page of jottings, and she went to the light to read it. She'd heard from Joe that he had sold one cow for a million, but thought it was a fluke. She read that he regularly sold them for that price and more.

"Wow! Uncle Mike'll have a jealous fit when he sees this! You must be a millionaire, Adam."

"Like most farmers, I'm land-rich, and fortunately not so cash-poor as most of my colleagues," he admitted. "But a sale isn't pure profit. It costs more than people realize to breed the cows and raise them, with vet fees and things."

"I'm glad you brought this. My article almost made your life seem like a fairy tale. That lovely life-style plus you're getting rich. Most farmers are having a rough time of it."

"Too rough. If they were wise they'd sell and get out. The small farm is no longer a good business venture. But there's more than money at stake, of course. It's a very satisfying life-style, if you don't mind hard work. As to my own 'fortune,' a million isn't what it used to be. And as I said, it's not pure profit by any means. In fact, I'm in debt to the bank for the breeding farm. We had to take out a mortgage to buy it. Things go wrong. Weather, disease, employee problems."

She looked up at that last item, to see if he meant her. He was looking at her uncertainly. He looked totally out of place in the small room. His broad shoulders and carved oak face needed the open spaces to appear at home.

"Throw in a hot French temper—" He shrugged his broad shoulders. A small smile lifted his lips. "Donna, I'm sorry," he said simply. "I was out of line, ripping up at you. I'd like you to come back."

"Yes, you were out of line. I wasn't making fun of you that night."

"I know. Do you think I haven't replayed those moments in my head a hundred times? I'm not as hard a man as you think." He looked, hoping she'd continue this line.

"And it *was* a family anniversary party," she said, rather sharply.

Adam batted his hand, to show he had dismissed all that. "I'd like you to work full-time. Then you could quit that supermarket job. You wouldn't have to be darting back and forth from Bayville at noon. Joe will show you the whole operation.''

So it was just a reliable farmhand he wanted, Donna thought. Well, she had no intention of making a career of farming. She didn't want to throw herself back into Adam's orbit, either, to have her heart battered again.

"Thanks, Adam, but I'm not really interested. The writing's going so well, I feel I'm near a breakthrough. The pay for the Samara article will allow me to hold off on a second job for a few weeks. I plan to keep my nose at the typewriter. If Mike likes the article, he might assign me another of the historical series. No one has done anything on the schools, for instance. I used to pass a little red brick schoolhouse on the way to Samara. The stone over the door says 1890, and it's still in use.''

They had their conversation standing in the living room. Adam wanted an excuse to sit down and stay awhile. He said, "I attended that school myself. I could tell you how it was twenty years ago, if that's any good to you.''

"It'd help, but before I waste your time with an interview, I'll check it out with Mike.''

"My evening's free,'' he said, glinting a hopeful smile at her.

Oh, no, he was starting it again. "I'm right in the middle of an outline.'' She looked impatiently at her typewriter, because she knew that if she went on looking into those smoky gray eyes, she'd do exactly what Adam wanted.

"I'm keeping you from work. Sorry.''

She began walking to the door. "Thanks for this info, Adam. I believe Mike plans to run the article on Saturday. Do you want to see the revisions before it goes to press?''

"I'm sure I can depend on you to do a good job. Good night.'' Then he turned and went out into the dark hallway.

Chapter Eleven

Donna went to the *Beacon* office with Jeanie the next morning to hand in her article on Samara. While waiting for Mike's verdict, she had a cup of coffee at Jeanie's desk.

"It won't take him long. He's a fast reader," Jeanie said. They talked for ten minutes, then Jeanie said, "I wish he'd hurry up. I should be hitting the road. I'm pounding on doors this morning trying to drum up new business."

"You don't have to wait."

"I'd like to hear the verdict. I can't imagine what's taking him so long. Unless—"

"Oh, Lord, he doesn't like it," Donna said. "It was too flowery."

"Worst-case scenario, a rewrite. Oh, well, I guess I really have to go. Good luck."

Donna waited another ten minutes, growing more uncertain by the moment. When Mike's secretary finally called her into Mike's office, she was prepared to hear the worst.

She looked at Mike who looked at her with sharp blue eyes. Her uncle was short and stout, with a red face and snow-white hair. He had not only his suits but also his shirts made to measure, and managed to convey an air of authority, despite his unprepossessing physique.

"A million bucks for one cow?" he asked, skewering her with a gimlet look. "You sure you got this figure right, Donna?"

"From the horse's mouth, Mike," she assured him.

He rubbed his fingers across his puffed pink cheeks. "I wonder now, how big a herd could a fellow raise on fifty acres?"

"Around fifty, I imagine," she said, doing a rough calculation. "Why do you ask, Mike?" This seemed an irrelevant question, since Samara had a lot more than fifty acres.

"Just curious." His jacket hung open. He stuck his thumbs into his waistband and walked to the window at a peculiar swaggering gait, toes pointed out.

Donna got the idea that he was putting himself into the role of Adam Challow. He stood at his office window, narrowing his eyes to slits as he gazed out at what he considered *his* city, with his hands on his hips. "Yup, it's a man's life on the farm," he said, in a strangely drawling voice. "Up at dawn, in the saddle—er, tractor—all day. Fresh air and sunshine. You did a good job on the background, Donna. It took me back to my youth."

"You liked the article, then?" she asked, holding her breath.

"It was good. In fact, it was better than good. It had—*feeling,*" he said. "Young Matt Hibbert, he says that's what wins rating points in TV. Our news pages have to be factual, but for a special feature like this, we want feeling. I pay on the day the article's printed."

She could hardly contain her elation. "That's great. I was wondering if you'd thought of doing anything on the old school system for this series, Mike," she said, striking while the iron was hot. She told him about the little red brick schoolhouse.

"Mrs. Addison ran that place when I was a tyke. We're talking half a century ago. She was all bone and gristle, that woman. Ruled two dozen of us with an iron fist and a wooden yardstick. I had my knuckles rapped by that lady more than once. You're really interested in taking the story on?"

"Yes," she said eagerly.

"You got it. Call the secretary at the local school board to see who's teaching there now. And while you're talking to the secretary, you might as well set up your interview with the chairman of the school board. You'll want to do some comparison with today's educational system. Be sure you include something on the working mothers. That's a big issue today."

"Leave it to me," she said, rising and collecting her purse. "When do you want it?"

"By the weekend, if you can swing it. It'll run a week Saturday. I can't run the church piece. I've had to ask the vicar for a rewrite. If I have to reach for my dictionary more than once, the article's too highbrow. Bear that in mind, Donna. This isn't a literary magazine. I write for plain folks. If you think of any other ideas, we'll talk. I haven't assigned the piece on hotels yet. Send in Eileen."

Donna went home, walking on clouds. Another article! That gave her another professional sale, and more important, two more weeks of not having to find a morning job. And maybe a third article on hotels. It also gave her an excuse to call Adam for that interview about his school days, but she'd wait and think about it. Uncle Mike's experiences would be better, as they went back farther. She set up an interview with the chairman of the local school board, and also got the name of the teacher who ran the little red brick schoolhouse. It was now a kindergarten school. That's something else that wasn't common in the old days. It would tie in with the working mothers aspect.

When Jeanie came home from work, she had some strange news to report. "I think Uncle Mike's flipped his lid," she said. "He's gone and bought himself a cowboy hat and boots. He looks really dumb, stomping around the office. He called me 'girl' twice. Do you think he's becoming senile?"

"Maybe it's the result of my article on Samara," Donna said with a smile. "I got the idea he was turning into a cowboy just before I left."

"He must be fixing for a shoot-out at the OK Corral. He was on the phone to town councillors all afternoon. They're discussing the rezoning of Highway 37 west of town this week. That's where Mike bought that land to build a condo."

Donna remembered Adam's speaking about it the night they went to the Bennets' barbecue. "The farmers there are dead set against it," she said. "Adam's organized a protest committee."

"That'd explain why Mike was phoning all the councillors."

"You mean bribing them?"

"I doubt if money changes hands. More like friendly persuasion. Mike has a monopoly on reporting the doings of the town council. And they'll be coming up for reelection this fall. They don't want any unflattering press at this time."

"That's not fair. No wonder Adam and the farmers despise Mike."

"Who he might be bribing is Adam Challow," Jeanie said uncertainly.

Donna blinked, trying to make sense of this. "You're crazy. He's the last man Mike would try that with."

"I know Eileen placed a call to Adam this afternoon. She told me at coffee break and warned me not to mention it to the others. She thought it was okay to tell me, since Mike's my uncle. And that's not all. She set up a meeting for Mike tonight at Samara."

"I don't believe this!"

"Adam was the one spearheading the farmers' movement to stop the rezoning. If the change goes through without any resistance, we'll know," Jeanie said. "Well, we'll have some pretty convincing circumstantial evidence, at least. Personally I don't think Mike has a chance. It's not as though Adam needs the money. According to your article, he's in clover financially. Of course, it isn't the highway east of town that Mike wants rezoned, so Adam's farm wouldn't be directly involved."

Donna gave an angry look to her cousin. "He'll fight it for his friends. The Bennets, and the other small farmers on that road."

"Maybe Adam's striking a deal that Mike won't develop anything east of town, if Adam doesn't fight the rezoning to the west."

Donna scoffed at her idea. Adam wasn't that selfish—was he? He had said that if those small farmers were wise they'd get out and cut their losses, though. He hadn't mentioned that in front of the farmers at the barbecue. And he wasn't as rich as one would think, either. He had a mortgage on the breeding farm. But Donna still couldn't believe that Adam would turn traitor on his friends for money or anything else. If his principles didn't stop him, his dislike of Mike Calvert would. But he agreed to meet Mike. At night. At Samara, where no one would see them. "When is the council meeting?" she asked.

"Tomorrow night at eight. It should be interesting. I'd like to go, but Doug has to cover the ballet school's summer review, though maybe I'll skip that," she said.

"Well, I'm going to that council meeting. I'll tell you what happens."

Donna was so upset at what Jeanie had said that she could hardly eat dinner. The more she thought about that meeting at Samara, the worse it looked for Adam. She acquitted him of selling out for money, but he'd do almost anything to protect Samara. A high rise across the road would certainly detract from its idyllic charm. Maybe that was what had convinced him. When Jeanie left with Doug at eight, Donna decided to call the farm. She'd use the school interview as an excuse.

At eight, she placed the call, and was surprised when Adam answered in person. She thought he'd be busy with Mike.

"Adam," she said, adopting a brightly impersonal tone. "Guess what. I got the school article. Are you still available for that interview?"

"Congratulations. I'm available any time."

"How about tonight?"

There was a little hesitation. "I have a business associate with me at the moment."

"I hope I'm not interrupting anything important?" she asked, her anger rising. She just knew Mike was there, right now.

"Not as important as seeing you," he replied, his voice warming. "I could be there by nine-thirty, if that's not too late?"

"That'll be fine. See you at nine-thirty," she said, and hung up.

So it was true, he *was* having a secret meeting with Mike, possibly to cut the ground out from under his friends' feet. Wasn't there anything she could do to stop this conspiracy? At least she could tell Adam Challow exactly what she thought of him. She'd give Mike a blast tomorrow, too, and if he took away the school story, so much the better. She didn't want to write for such a sleazy employer, anyway.

She had an hour and a half before Adam was coming. He probably thought she would greet him with cold wine and warm words. Well, he'd have a surprise. She didn't do a thing to make herself attractive. She had a shower and didn't even use the hair dryer. She just combed her hair straight back and didn't put on any makeup. A faded denim skirt and an old college jersey were good enough for a miserable wretch like Adam.

When he came, he looked surprised to see her dressed so casually. He was wearing a business shirt and tailored trousers. He had shaved, and his hair was slicked down. Donna sensed an air of excitement about him. His smoky eyes had turned to shimmering gray crystals, and his lips were curved in an incipient smile.

"Am I early?" he asked, glancing at his watch. "Blame it on my eagerness to see you."

She had to steel herself to withstand that smile, which still had the power to melt her insides, even knowing what he had done. "Right on time. You didn't have to dress up, Adam. But then you mentioned a business meeting. I hope my call didn't distract you."

"I always find you distracting, Donna," he said. The smile grew wider. "But the meeting was successful. I try to put business before pleasure."

"Or first things first," she said snidely. Donna still found him dangerously attractive, but she schooled herself to mistrust this traitor, who had been born with the kind of rugged good looks that simulated integrity and inspired trust.

"Shall we sit down?" she said, walking toward the love seat sofa. A full-size one would have overwhelmed the small room.

"Is there any reason we can't have this interview over a few drinks somewhere?" he suggested.

"Like you said, business before pleasure. I like to keep a clear head for business," she said, and sat down primly, with both feet on the floor.

"In that case, I'll keep my distance—until the interview is over."

This bantering flirtation was accompanied by a smile that was hard to resist. Adam sat on the far end of the sofa. He settled in comfortably, with one hand stretched along the sofa back. His fingers brushed her shoulder. When he turned to look at her, a smile began in his eyes and slowly spread downward. It was an intimate smile that stirred strange yearnings inside her. "Ready when you are," he said softly. But that gentle voice wasn't talking about business. It spoke of more romantic things. "Do you want to ask questions, or shall I just reminisce?"

"Let's play question and answer," she suggested, mimicking his smile.

"Anything you want to know, just ask."

"Gee, that's kind of like interviewing Einstein," she said, with a mocking smile.

"Just so you don't quiz me on the theory of relativity. Won't you want a pencil and paper to take notes?"

"My memory's pretty good, Adam."

"So's mine," he murmured. His eyes suggested what he was remembering. "Fire away."

She took a steadying breath to keep her own memories at bay and said, in a perfectly polite voice, "All right. Let's begin with your meeting with Mike Calvert at Samara tonight. The timing strikes me as pertinent. The night before the town council meeting to discuss rezoning Highway 37. You got any comments on that?"

His black brows drew together in a quick frown. "How the devil did you learn about that? Mike said he didn't tell anyone."

"A reporter likes to keep her sources private. Was the meeting about the rezoning?"

"What's that got to do with my school days?" he asked in confusion.

"I brought you here under false pretenses."

Adam wasn't angry yet, but he was bewildered. "I suspected as much, but I must say, I placed a more romantic interpretation on the invitation."

"Oh, really? You thought I wanted to seduce you?"

"My hopes didn't soar quite that high."

"Like I said, this interview is strictly business. So you admit you and Mike discussed the rezoning of Highway 37?"

Adam drew his stretched arm away from Donna and assumed a more rigid posture. "Is this some kind of game?"

"That's right. Twenty questions." She rose to her feet, all pretense dropped. Her eyes shot sparks as she stared down at him. "Why did you do it? Why did you go along with that crook? You have never had a good word to say for Mike Calvert."

"I was happy to discover he's not as bad as I thought. He's a reasonable man."

"You just did it to make sure Samara isn't invaded by condos," she accused.

"What's wrong with that? You know my feelings about the encroaching development. I thought you shared them."

"Only to a point, Adam. I don't share your selfish view of sacrificing the interests of old friends just to save my own hide. I think what you did is despicable."

Adam's temper rose in parallel with her voice. "Mike had already bought the land," he said, reining in his ire.

"The land bordering the Bennets' farm? Is that the land you're talking about?"

"Of course. I was beginning to think we were talking about two different things. I don't see what you're so mad about."

"How can you stand there and say that to me?" she demanded, her voice high with disbelief. "All that tub-thumping about saving the farmlands for the farmers! As long as Mike doesn't build his high rises within sight of Samara, you don't give a damn. You were just using the friendship of your neighbors to secure your own selfish interest."

Adam was on his feet now, too, towering menacingly above her. "Just what, exactly, are you accusing me of?"

"Of striking a deal with Mike that you won't fight his rezoning of the west strip as long as he doesn't build east of town."

Adam stared at her as if she were insane. When he spoke, his voice was filled with disbelief. "So that's what this is all about. If you're planning to write this up for the paper, I suggest you get your facts straight, lady, or you'll find yourself hit with a libel suit."

Donna's uncertainty began to slip, but a hasty review of the situation told her there was no other explanation. Adam was bluffing. "Do you deny it, then?"

"Categorically."

He spoke so positively that her doubts changed to a certainty that she was wrong. "Then what is going on? Why was Mike phoning all the councillors today? And why this highly secret meeting with you?"

Adam looked at her for a long moment, trying to decide whether to explain or just leave. The inferences of her accusations were so insulting that he could hardly control himself. Better leave. "Why don't you ask your uncle, since you obviously don't trust my word?" He turned on his heel and strode angrily toward the door.

Donna watched, with her heart sinking into her feet. What had she done? She ran after him. "Adam, I don't understand. I didn't mean to accuse you—"

He stopped at the door and leveled a dark gaze at her. "That's exactly what you did mean," he said, in a voice of chilling disdain. "Without one iota of proof, with nothing but the suspicions of your own lurid imagination, you accused me of being a turncoat to my lifelong friends, for my own selfish interest. Can you *really* think I would do that? My God, I thought I was beginning to understand you."

Donna felt as if she had been kicked in the stomach by Rambo. The wind had gone out of her, and when she tried to speak, no words came. Not even, "I'm sorry." She just looked on helplessly as Adam opened the door and stalked out. She had never seen him so furious.

Where had she gone wrong? What *could* Mike Calvert and Adam Challow possibly have to discuss except Mike's real estate development? Yet Adam had denied it categorically. And she knew he was telling the truth. She had always found it hard to believe he would do what she suspected. Why hadn't she made certain before accusing him?

Jeanie told her why when she returned an hour later and listened to Donna's disjointed tale.

"It's that vivid Gemini imagination. You're too quick in making judgments. Inclined to go to extremes."

"It's not imagination that Mike was at Samara tonight. Adam admitted it."

"I found out why. At least Doug found out. We met one of the councillors in the restaurant. Mike's not going to build on his fifty acres. He's going to set up a dairy farm. He just decided today. He's withdrawn his application for a zone change. That's why he was phoning the mayor and his friend on the town council, to notify them, since it was on the agenda for tomorrow night's meeting."

"Mike turning farmer? I can't believe it."

"It's all your fault. It was your article on Samara that gave him the idea. I think the million bucks for a really first-rate cow had something to do with it, but it wasn't just that. He's got more money than even Dora could ever spend. It's probably a mid-life crisis. He's looking for emotional fulfillment. Back to his roots."

Donna listened and found it easy to believe after the way Mike had acted in his office that morning. "And Adam's going to help him set up the farm?"

"Yeah, Mike's going to buy some cows or calves from Adam. Isn't that a kicker? Those two have always been at loggerheads. They say politics makes strange bedfellows, but greed runs it a close second. I mean Mike's greed," she added, when Donna bristled. "I was wondering if Adam went along with it because of you." She examined her cousin with brightly curious eyes.

"Me? What do you mean?"

"Well, Mike's part of your family," Jeanie said. "The only part of it in the immediate area. If Adam was serious about you, he wouldn't want to be on bad terms with your family. It's just an idea."

It was an idea that Donna could believe. Adam had said something of the sort when he offered to go to the anniversary party with her. And she had put him off. Why had she done it? That was really the beginning of all her troubles with Adam.

He had seen her coming home with Matt and jumped to the conclusion that she was laughing at him behind his back. She had been so angry with him, and now she had done the same thing herself. Jumped to the wrong conclusion.

Why was it that two people in love couldn't communicate? She knew that she was in love with Adam, and his efforts to please her hinted that he felt the same way. She had joked a bit about Adam's being a farmer. Maybe he was more sensitive than she thought. But what was her excuse for mistrusting him? He just seemed too good to be true, and all the evidence had seemed to be against him.

"So, what are you going to do about it?" Jeanie asked. She unscrewed a bottle of ginger ale, poured two glasses and handed Donna one.

"What can I do? I've made a complete fool of myself, Jeanie."

"I should think a highly imaginative and sincere Gemini with a magnetic personality and not bad looks could do something to convince him she's sorry."

"Convince a stubborn Capricorn who resists changing course?"

Jeanie smiled mischievously. "The stars suggest, they don't compel. Besides, Capricorns love overcoming obstacles. If he loves you, he'll meet you half way."

"But he doesn't love me. He thinks I'm a jerk." She frowned and said, "What do you mean, not bad-looking?"

"The way you look tonight, that's a compliment, babe. What were you trying to do, turn him off?"

"No, I was just showing him I didn't give a damn how I looked for him. And don't call me babe."

"Hey, don't kill the messenger."

They drank their ginger ale while mulling over the situation. The only hope Donna could see was that she and Adam were both doing some business with Mike now, and they might meet from time to time.

"Mike will probably do a series of articles on his new farm," Jeanie said. "He always gives himself lots of publicity. Since he thinks you're an expert on dairy farming, he might ask you to do the writing. Your research could take you to Samara."

"Probably, might, could—that's pretty iffy."

"I was just trying to be supportive, since your own imagination seems to have run dry. If it were me, I wouldn't sit on my duff whining while a great guy like Adam Challow got away from me. But of course Donna's shy," she said, sticking her finger in her mouth and making a shy face.

"What would you do?"

"I'd kick-start my pursuing instincts. I'd buy a lasso and go after him," Jeanie said. "Rope him and brand him." Then she took her glass to the sink and went to prepare for bed.

Donna sat on alone in the small living room, wondering what she could do to win Adam back. A lasso and a branding iron weren't her style, but sitting back and letting her pride keep her mute wasn't going to work. Maybe Jeanie was right. Sometimes shyness was just a socially acceptable name for pride. Well, it was time to swallow her pride and turn pursuer.

Chapter Twelve

"**I**'m going to lasso that critter, rope it and brand it," Donna announced at breakfast the next morning.

"About time. I'll lend you my lasso," Jeanie grinned.

"I'm not talking about Adam."

"Then who?"

"I'm not talking about a person. I mean the assignment on Mike's dairy farm. Those articles are *mine*. I'm going down to the *Beacon* with you this morning, and I won't leave until I have a signed contract."

"Mike doesn't sign contracts with employees. *I* hoped you'd intended to use the articles as an excuse to see Adam."

"The idea has occurred to me," Donna said, with a grin. "I'll put on lipstick and perfume before I go."

Jeanie glanced at her watch. "You'd better get cracking, then. I'll be leaving in five minutes. Or will you be driving the van?"

"I'll go with you. If Adam's there, I want an excuse to get into his wagon."

"You're beginning to get the idea. I never saw you scheme for a man before, Donna," Jeanie said approvingly.

"You ain't seen nothing yet."

As soon as they reached the *Beacon,* Donna marched into Mike's office and began laying siege to him. "Mike, you have to let me do a series on your new enterprise," she said. "Bayville will want to read all about it."

Mike's cowboy hat sat on his desk. He leaned back in his chair with his booted feet on the desk. His jacket was off, and he wore a plaid shirt. A string tie with metal clips on the end hung at his throat.

"I was planning to do a write-up," he admitted. "I figured my head writer could handle it."

"Does he know as much about dairy farming as I do?" she said. Her air of certainty suggested infinite familiarity with the trade.

"You did a good job on the Samara article," he admitted doubtfully.

Donna was prepared to use every weapon in her arsenal. This was war. "And I'm family," she reminded him. "Your farm means a lot to me, too. I'd really put my heart into it."

Mike nodded complacently. "There's something in what you say, girl. Your pa and me, we were raised on that bit of land."

Donna opened her lips to remind him that the old homestead was several miles farther west but caught herself in time. "I spent many a happy summer on the old homestead myself, Mike. I'd sure appreciate seeing the place again."

He glanced at the electric clock over his door. "Eleven o'clock at the Bar Beacon ranch, then." She blinked in confusion. "That's what I'm calling it. Because of my newspaper."

"Eleven o'clock it is," she said.

"I'll be meeting young Challow there. He's offered to give me the advantage of his expertise." Donna heard this with anxious elation. "I was planning a series of articles actually," Mike continued. "And a regular Saturday feature on the farming community in general. They don't get their due. I'll have to hire another reporter. You interested, girl?"

"Is that a firm offer? It'll mean quitting my job at the supermarket."

"What's a Calvert doing behind a counter, anyway?" he grumbled. "Yes, it's firm," he said, and mentioned the salary.

Donna didn't argue. It was plenty more than she made at the supermarket. Jeanie was on the phone as she left. Donna gave a big grin and the thumbs-up sign, and hurried on.

She had to ask for time off at the supermarket, and also gave her notice. Since she was part-time help, they didn't expect her to stay two weeks. The manager knew of her writing ambitions and was happy for her.

Her heart pounded erratically as she prepared for the meeting at Bar Beacon. She wasn't a farmhand now, and she didn't have to wear jeans and boots. She would wear the same fashionable striped dress she'd worn to the *Beacon*. Her heels would be a nuisance in the country. In fact, they would require a man's arm to help her over the rough terrain. So much the better. Adam had seen her in boots and jeans too often.

She fussed over her hair, and in the end tied a ribbon around it, since the wind would destroy any hairdo she attempted. She put on her gold hoop earrings and the little tennis bracelet Jeanie had given her. At the last minute, she remembered to take a notepad and pen. The van coughed and spluttered and finally decided to oblige her by turning over its engine. She didn't drive to the Bar Beacon but to the newspaper office to hitch a ride with Uncle Mike. If, by any chance, Adam was coming to town, she meant to ride back with *him*.

Mike didn't seem to notice that she was supposed to meet him at the farm. He was happy to have an audience for his dreams as they drove out of town.

"This is just what's been missing in my life," he confided. "The old cliché that 'money's nice, but it doesn't buy happiness' is true. I mean to build Dora and me a ranch house and sell off the city place. We'll get back to the soil. Dora's going to raise chickens," he smiled. "That little woman surprised the daylights out of me. She was tickled pink with the idea of farming."

He seemed sincere, even if he did go a little overboard with his accent. Donna encouraged him. "I'm sure you'll both enjoy it, Mike. It's very satisfying work."

She spotted Adam's yellow station wagon as they stopped at the road into the farm. He wasn't in it, but they soon spotted him farther off, looking over the land. His tall, straight body stood out like an exclamation point against the horizon. This open country seemed his natural element, with the limitless sky above and the fields stretching all around. Then he turned and saw them. Donna noticed that he was wearing sunglasses. They added an air of mystery to his sun-bronzed face.

"A fine figure of a man," Mike said forlornly. "I mean to shake off a few pounds. Cut back on the Scotch for starters. G'day, Adam," he called.

Adam's heart gave a lurch as he recognised Donna. Now what the devil was she doing here? Excitement mingled with anger in his breast as he strode to meet them. He noticed immediately that she had changed her style. And her expression. She zapped him with a smile that would melt the polar ice caps.

"Hi, Adam," she said. "I'm going to do some articles on Mike's new farm. And farming in general later on."

"No place for a Calvert, hawking beans and cabbages," Mike said. He strolled toward the house. It was a dilapidated clapboard with the front door hanging loose and half the windows out. He meant to tear it down.

"Congratulations," Adam said. "This'll do your career some good."

She gazed hard at his dark glasses, wishing he'd take them off. "Yes, that too," she replied enigmatically.

That *too?* Wasn't that the whole point of it? It sounded as if she had some ulterior motive, some motive that involved him, but he could hardly believe that Donna was flirting with him. He was so excited by the way she was smiling at him that he wasn't thinking quite straight.

"I was hoping I could tap into your expertise for some of the articles," she said. "If you can forgive me for last night, that is." She paused a moment and then said, "I'm sorry, Adam. I should have known better."

Her flirtatious manner had changed subtly as they talked. It was all gone now. Her voice resonated with sincerity. He felt himself respond instinctively to her new mood.

"No hard feelings. We all make mistakes," he said.

"Yes, especially when we're emotionally involved." It was as close as she could come to telling him how she felt.

Adam swallowed a lump in his throat. "Are you saying what I think you're saying, Donna?" he asked. His hands seized hers. "This isn't like you, somehow."

"Sometimes a gal's got to do what a gal's got to do," she said, and looked for his reaction.

Adam quickly adopted the same playful spirit. "You sure look mighty purty, Miss Calvert, ma'am."

"I reckon you look pretty good yourself behind those shades."

He slowly took them off and slid them into his shirt pocket. His smoky eyes were brimming with love and laughter. "Do you think we could get out of here? I'd like to—I think you know what I'd like to do."

His smoldering eyes, his husky voice, his whole body sent the message. "I just got hired this morning. I can't goof off already. But Mike has a meeting at noon..." she said, and looked an invitation at him.

"You have to be at the supermarket at two," he reminded her.

Her eyes never left his as she replied with meaningful deliberation, "I quit. I've burned a few bridges behind me. I figured it was time to quit playing it safe."

"I can't speak for your job at the *Beacon*, but whatever caused this change, you're safe with me, Donna."

A dizzying bubble of happiness swelled in her. "Just as long as I'm with you, I don't much care whether I'm safe or not."

While Adam was still reeling with disbelief, Mike called Adam from across the field. "What do you think of this shambles, Adam?" He pointed to the derelict house. "I was figuring to rip her down."

They turned to join Mike. Adam automatically put his hand on Donna's elbow to guide her through the long grass. The three of them walked over the land, with Adam suggesting the best spots for pasture and crops, and discussing fences. It was twelve-thirty when they left.

"You want a lift back to town, girl?" Mike asked.

She looked at Adam. "I'll drive Donna home," he said.

"Right. A good chance to clarify any little details for the article," Mike said. He glanced at his limousine. "This gas guzzler will have to go. I figure I'll need a pickup truck." He tipped his hat, got in and drove off for his appointment with the truck dealer.

Adam and Donna walked slowly, hand in hand, to his wagon and drove into town. They waited until they had gained the privacy of her apartment before discussing their situation.

"I guess I have some explaining to do," she said, when they were sitting on the little sofa of her living room.

"You forgive me for leaping to the wrong conclusion the night you were with your cousin, and I'll forgive you for thinking I was a jerk and a schemer."

"Shake, partner," she said, playfully shaking his hand. His fingers closed warmly over hers. "I don't know how I could ever have believed it of you for a minute. I could hardly believe it."

"I can only give my reasons. I knew you were ten times too good for me, and I was just waiting for the bottom to fall out of my dream. When you're waiting for something awful to happen, the anxiety gets so intense you make it happen, just to have it done with."

"I know what you mean. It's almost a relief when my articles come thumping back to me with the rejection letter, and I can go on with the next one."

Adam shook his head ruefully. "And to think, I thought you were a spoiled little rich girl." His fingers toyed with her tennis bracelet. At close range, he could see that it was costume jewelry. "And I still loved you," he said.

In the shadowed room, his eyes were a stormy Atlantic gray as they gazed into hers. "I still loved you, even when I thought you were a jerk," she admitted. "Maybe that's why we were both so angry. I mean we were angry with ourselves, as well as each other."

His arm stole around her waist and drew her against him. "Let's dissect this relationship another time," he said, nibbling at her jaw and sending feathery tingles down her spine. "I have to be at the breeding farm half an hour ago."

"Oh, I'm keeping you from work!" she said breathlessly.

"Mmm," he murmured, his lips grazing across her cheek to find her lips and assault them with a ruthless kiss.

Her arms went around him, savoring the taut sinews and masculine strength of his muscled back. Her breasts melted against his hard body. As the kiss deepened, she felt a heat growing within her as feverish longing ripened to desire. She knew Adam felt it, too. His hands moved possessively over her back, taking her measure, and claiming her for his own.

When she felt she was on the verge of suffocation, Adam raised his head and drew a shuddering sigh. His lips opened in a gentle smile, and he kissed her again, slowly, thoroughly, with his tongue performing sensuous strokes that left her dazed.

She drew back. "Adam, you're going to be late for your appointment," she said.

"Very late," he agreed, and pulled her down beside him on the sofa. His hands traced her outline, lingering on the thrust of her breasts, and clinging to her small waist. When he reached her lips, he pulled her snugly against him. "Very late," he repeated, moving his lips against the nape of her neck and demolishing her self-control. "I wouldn't be here, doing this, if I wasn't crazy about you, Donna. Is it too early to ask you to marry me?"

"Maybe you should give me a chance to tell you how I feel," she suggested. His eyes widened in alarm. "Same way," she said. "Now you can ask me to marry you."

"I want very much for you to be my wife."

"I'd like that, Adam," she said simply.

They jumped up in alarm when a key sounded in the lock. "It must be Jeanie!" she exclaimed. "What's she doing here? She never comes home for lunch."

"Yoo, hoo! Can I come in?" Jeanie called discreetly from the hallway when she saw the lights within.

"Of course," Donna called, trying to keep her voice calm. "Adam was just leaving," she added, to remind him of his appointment.

"Don't let me interrupt anything," Jeanie said, slipping inside. "I just came home to change. I spilled coffee all over my blouse at lunch." She disappeared into the bedroom.

Donna accompanied Adam to the door. "See you tonight?" he said, cupping her chin for a kiss.

"What time?"

"Sevenish. We'll go out for a celebration dinner. A double celebration, your job and our engagement."

"Right, but not in that order. First things first."

She gave him a quick kiss on the lips, and more or less shoved him out the door.

As soon as she heard the door close, Jeanie came running out, slipping her arms into a fresh blouse. "What was that all about?" she demanded.

"I'm engaged!" Donna said, and began to literally jump for joy.

"And you got the job! Congratulations, girl. This is a four-star day. I knew Adam wouldn't give up. Capricorns are very persistent."

"So are Geminis. I practically courted him. Me, imagine!"

"You Geminis can be clever," Jeanie allowed.

"And you said our signs weren't favorable."

"I also said the stars lead, they don't compel. I'll have to study your aspects and see when is a propitious time for you to get married."

"It better be soon. Capricorns may be patient, but we Geminis like to move quickly."

"I had a feeling you were putting the moves on Adam," Jeanie laughed. "I told you you should be more aggressive."

"I wasn't aggressive. I just told him the truth. Mind you, it felt pretty aggressive," she admitted.

"And pretty good, huh?"

"I could get used to it."

Jeanie buttoned her blouse. "I better hurry. Mike's having a roundup of all the staff today to announce some changes. He'll be spending less time at the paper, so he'll have to delegate some of his work."

"That's nice," Donna said, obviously not listening. She went to the sofa and sat, hugging a cushion and smiling dreamily. *Mrs. Adam Challow.* For better, for worse. For richer, for poorer. Forever.

* * * * *

LOVE AND
THE CAPRICORN MAN

by Wendy Corsi

January is a time for fresh starts, and the conscientious Capricorn man will probably have a long list of New Year's resolutions ready at the stroke of midnight! Topping the list for the Capricorn bachelor will be his determination to get married. This traditional man is always seeking security and is happiest as a husband. The married Capricorn man will promise to make an effort to spend less time working and more time wooing his wife with his favorite old-fashioned, romantic standbys: red roses and champagne!

In For Richer, for Poorer, Capricorn Adam Challow resolved to settle his differences with Gemini Donna Calvert. What New Year's resolutions would a Capricorn man make for you?

The free-spirited *Aries* woman may baffle buttoned-down Capricorn, but her boundless energy appeals to his ambitious nature. She's bursting with sunny optimism, and hopefully, it's contagious! In the new year, workaholic Capricorn should schedule time to relax and indulge in the occasional long weekend with his lighthearted female. After all, all work and no play...

Controlling Capricorn may initially mistake the ultra-feminine *Taurus* woman for a marshmallow, but he'll soon realize she's one tough cookie! She's impressed by his full-speed-ahead efforts to win her heart; he appreciates her cautious character. To make the year ahead *really* harmonious, he can try to feel flattered rather than annoyed whenever her famous jealous streak surfaces!

Domestically inclined *Cancer* is the ideal match for traditional Capricorn. Her taste may be a trifle expensive for this frugal man, but thanks to his financial artistry, he can probably afford the quality she craves. He'd be wise this New Year's Eve to promise to pay extra attention to his Cancer woman from now on—she's quick to feel neglected when he's engrossed in his work!

The *Leo* woman loves to be the center of attention—something the more reserved Capricorn man tends to forget. She makes her many successes seem so effortless that he may forget to compliment her—he's too busy wondering how she does it! This year, he'll keep in mind that a little praise will keep his lady positively purring.

A *Virgo* woman is sensible, dependable and financially savvy...sound like anyone you know? Yes, Capricorns and Virgos are cut from the same cosmic cloth, and this devoted duo is a safe bet for longevity. When he's drawing up his list of resolutions, the Capricorn man should remember that the Virgo woman doesn't appreciate his constructive criticism, but with a little tenderness, she thrives!

Charming *Libra* is the social butterfly of the Zodiac, but surprisingly, she's the marrying kind...just like Capricorn. But this January, the Capricorn man must realize he'll *never* be able to clip her wings. He'll have to come up with more creative ways to prove that a quiet night home alone can be anything but dull.

The *Scorpio* woman's trademark is her passionate nature. On the surface, mild-mannered Capricorn may not seem to be a likely match, but he, too, has a sensual side. This New Year's Day, Capricorn will be daring and reveal his sexy nature... behind closed doors, of course!

Impulsive *Sagittarius* and pragmatic Capricorn see life from opposite sides, but when they finally manage to meet in the middle, the balance is blissful! When Capricorn's calendar signals a fresh start, he should vow to stop trying to change his lady love and accept her independent spirit as is—the challenge will be worthwhile!

When *two* steadfast *Capricorns* come together, they're sure to fall into traditional masculine and feminine roles, much to their mutual delight! He'll strive to keep life on an even keel, but eventually, even these two unadventurous souls may find their days too predictable. As January approaches, they'd do well to consider spicing up the next twelve months by shedding a few inhibitions!

Outrageous *Aquarius* can be easily distracted but secretly longs to be pinned down. Earnest Capricorn is just the man for the job, though he'll be taken aback by his mate's many eccentricities! When the clock strikes twelve this New Year's Eve, Capricorn should catch her by surprise with a toe-curling kiss... then vow to keep her guessing in the coming year!

Intuitive, dramatic *Pisces* is a blatant romantic who revels in being needed, and her secret fantasy is to be rescued and protected! The ideal hero for this winsome woman? Courtly Capricorn, of course. His ideal New Year's resolution? To take time from his hectic work schedule and call several times a day...just to say "I love you!"

NORA ROBERTS

Love has a language all its own, and for centuries, flowers have symbolized love's finest expression. Discover the language of flowers—and love—in this romantic collection of 48 favorite books by bestselling author Nora Roberts.

Starting in February 1992, two titles will be available each month at your favorite retail outlet.

In February, look for:

Irish Thoroughbred, Volume #1
The Law Is A Lady, Volume #2

Collect all 48 titles and become fluent in the Language of Love.

LOL192

THE LANGUAGE of LOVE

Silhouette Romance®

LONG, TALL TEXANS

DONAVAN
Diana Palmer

Diana Palmer's bestselling LONG, TALL TEXANS series continues with DONAVAN....

From the moment elegant Fay York walked into the bar on the wrong side of town, rugged Texan Donavan Langley knew she was trouble. But the lovely young innocent awoke a tenderness in him that he'd never known...and a desire to make her a proposal she couldn't refuse....

Don't miss DONAVAN by Diana Palmer, the ninth book in her LONG, TALL TEXANS series. Coming in January...only from Silhouette Romance.

LTT192

Silhouette Special Edition®

salutes

MOMENTS OF GLORY

from Lindsay McKenna

In a country torn with conflict, in a time of bitter passions, these brave men and women wage a war against all odds... and a timeless battle for honor, for fleeting moments of glory, for the promise of enduring love.

February: RIDE THE TIGER (#721) Survivor Dany Villard is wise to the love-'em-and-leave-'em ways of war, but wounded hero Gib Ramsey swears she's captured his heart... forever.

March: ONE MAN'S WAR (#727) The war raging inside brash and bold Captain Pete Mallory threatens to destroy him, until Tess Ramsey's tender love guides him toward peace.

April: OFF LIMITS (#733) Soft-spoken Marine Jim McKenzie saved Alexandra Vance's life in Vietnam; now he needs her love to save his honor....

SEMG-1